ALL-Ways the Rebel

Escape into Two World Wars

by Al & Pete Allaway

PublishAmerica
Baltimore

ISBN: 1-4241-9334-6
PUBLISHED BY PUBLISHAMERICA, LLLP
www.publishamerica.com
Baltimore

Printed in the United States of America

Foreword

Basil Lawrence "Pete" Allaway (1899-1962) served in both world wars, first in the United States Navy as a yeoman chief petty officer aboard the U.S.S. *Huron,* an impounded German cruise liner that was converted for troop transport, mostly between New York and France. In the Second World War, as a U. S. Army corporal in Assam, India, supporting the construction of the Ledo Road into Burma. The new road was to supply help to the Chinese in order to repel the Japanese invaders.

These are his tales of escape from reality and moral responsibility, told with some regard for fact, but mostly with lighthearted humor. It is a work of imagination and fiction, liberally sprinkled with some of Pete's poetry. History buffs and scholars will appreciate the good parallel with the time-lines of the two wars, with Prohibition and the Great Depression. The story covers with precision the places Pete was sent and most of what he accomplished (or failed to accomplish).

Many of the incidents I have concocted about him and his World War One Navy have been recalled from doubtful and failing memory. As a result, this work must be listed as "fiction" instead of the true war memoir it was intended to be.

Pete was always a rebel. Between the two wars, while paying society some owed restitution, he acknowledged this fault in a sonnet written to his first of four wives.

> A rebel at my birth, how should I know
> How futile was the urge that made me stray
> Away from you and down the broad highway,
> Drawn like a moth along its licensed glow?
> But I was young and would have it so,
> I thought of living once to stray and yearn

For vicious freedom, now I would return
Where birds sing sweetly, and where flowers grow.
***
I am a rebel still, but I rebel
Against rebellion now, and I believe
In faith and love again, in hearts that grieve,
And I'm afraid of freedom—and of hell!
Let me return to your sweet shrine of charms
And lose my freedom in your clinging arms!

"Pearl," "Winnie," "Shimmy Immy," "Popeye Pete," "Putzi" and "Gomer Fudd" are fictional names, but represent the people who suffered the separation between friends and lovers, caused by the two wars.

Pete's World War II letters (to Putzi) and sonnets have been in storage, only recently surfacing. Please note that I have transcribed his grammatical errors, punctuation and strange spelling exactly as written, believing it was his intention to use a homespun literary style. If the movie character Forrest Gump had been around during the two world wars, one could almost suspect plagiarism.

When time-line gaps needed filling, I liberally concocted myth and legend, sometimes using experiences from my own military service. Are you, the reader, up to the challenge of separating fact from fiction? *Time makes myths of us all.*

Finally, be prepared for those obsequious time flashbacks; there is one in each chapter, adequately identified. Each chapter starts with the 1940s *"Letters to Putzi"* then flashes back to a parallel event in the 1920s Navy.

There is a smattering of real history and lifestyles of people who lived in the early twentieth century, through the "Great War for Civilization" and leading up to the terrible financial "crashes" of the late 1920s.

People lived and loved then, much as they do today.

R. M. "Al" Allaway
Yakima, Washington,
June 20, 2007

Chapter 1

Army Draft
September 15, 1942

Dear Putzi:

Would you believe it? I got a letter from President Roosevelt this week honestly. It was addressed to Mr. Gomer Oliver Fudd, Sunnyside, Washington and sent down here by the P.M. It said, "Greetings, a committee of your neighbors have decided to put you in the army."

Right at first I was very pleased but then I begun to think that maybe it was a scheme to give some of them fat lady welders a better chance.

Of course I didn't tell you that I was welding. The other night I was setting on a stool and sputtering like the old harry when someone tapped me on the shoulder. Well, it was only the timekeeper but I jumped so hard that I burnt my shirt and tipped over the stool onto his foot and did he squawk. Oh boy. Well, afterwards I told the boss about my letter and he shook hands with me and said that it was a great loss to the shipyards as they were now engaged in making landing craft tanks which won't be heard of 'till next year. But he was sure that I would be an addition to the army of some kind he says.

Also, I guess I forgot to tell you that I got tired of pitching hay and horse droppings so that's why I ending up welding down there in Vancouver last month.

When I read about my neighbors being so considerate of me I thought it would be a good idea to go and see them so a few days later I took a autobust to Sunnyside. The first morning I was there I went up to their office and talked to a girl kinda oldish like. She said that it was all just symbolical and told me to be at the railway station at 8:45 PM in the evening with nothing but a toothbrush. Well, I got there with my toothbrush but I had clothes on and something else as you will soon see.

After I left that office I repaired to a beer joint for a couple and met Tennessee which we used to call old Mr. Boston, and he bought me a couple of quick ones and then took me to his cabin where we met several people who had some whisky and stuff and when I woke up I was alone by myself with a terrible thirst. After several minutes of debate among myself I decided to seek out the nearest likker store which was my downfall. And I don't mean maybe or perhaps. All of a sudden I heard a train whistle.

Now there ain't many trains at Sunnyside it being on a wye of a jerk-water branch. So I looked at my Ingersoll and found out it was 9:05 pm in the evening and that I was sitting along side of the likker store in an alley. So I jumped and ran and when I got near the RR station I skidded in the gravel and slid on my face for several feet.

On the railroad platform I met the first of my good neighbors. He roared, "Are you Fudd?"

And I said, "Yes."

And he said, "Get the hell on that train which is awaiting for you." Well dear, that is the first time a train waited 20 minutes for yours truly. So when I got on the boys wiped the blood from off my face and we repaired to the ladies room where we sang songs to the accompaniment of a quart of whisky. Some time during the night they poured me into a upper birth and when I tried to jump out in the morning I found my ankle swelled up like my head felt so I could hardly walk. Anyhow we were going someplace.

About 1:00 am in the next morning we arrived at Salt Lake City, Utah and we were loaded into trucks like cattle and hauled to Fort Douglas which is on a high hill over the town. We were all marched into a building where they gave us a little book and told us to take all our clothes off. After that they gave us a test to see if we were all pure. Hoping you are the same, I remain,

Yours truly, *Gomer Fudd*

P.S. I had a dream that sorta paralleled this, and reminded me of that other war, which I also served in and it went something like this:

#

8

A War to End All Wars
April 6, 1917

There was a secret pleasure in knowing that in two days I would be eighteen years old. It seemed like there was supposed to be some sort of a magic spell that would happen and I would suddenly be transformed into a "man." I used to think that happened when Ma gave me my first pair of long trousers, but that had turned out to be a big disappointment.

"Basil," her voice would thunder up the stairs, "get out there and slop the hogs."

"Awr, Ma," says I, "I'm grown-up now. That's kid stuff. Why can't Chris or Hillary do it?"

Ma was a tiny little woman, but she had a stamina of steel, further hardened by birthing eleven of us and she quickly settled the question beyond any further argument, that chores would be done, regardless of one's head swollen with self-importance. Long pants didn't mean a thing.

Now I was about to climb to a higher plateau; one of significantly more stature. I had my high school diploma in hand and felt like conquering the world. Any life would be better than continuing to be an Iowa farmer. Such pleasing accomplishments did not come cheaply, however. The world in 1917 was in turmoil, especially over in Europe, and any lad approaching maturity would have to consider joining up to defend his country if war ever came to the United States.

So far, President Woodrow Wilson and the Congress had kept us out of the fray by maintaining shaky neutrality. It had been three years since the war clouds had gathered in Austria, France, England and Germany. We had been lucky up until then.

My mind, however, had been far from the political problems across the seas. That conflict seemed too far away to be any real threat. Besides, there had been a brand-new dolly in town who created a new challenge, a girl that I must conquer!

April the sixth dawned like any other spring day in eastern Iowa. When that danged ol' Charlie interrupted my dreams, I flinched at his crowing. I'd like to pitch him into the cooking pot!

The house was too quiet; no slamming doors. No hollering, no stomping down the stairs. Then, I remembered that it was Saturday and most of the spring plowing had been done, so we'd be getting a day off because it was still too risky to plant any seeds. The second thing I noticed, was my hung-over headache. The night before, I had tried to woo that pretty little filly into a date at the church social, but she turned me down flat. So I took out my revenge on a bottle of whiskey. Ma would really croak me if she knew. The third thing to pass through my foggy brain was that it was my birthday. Holy smokes! I was eighteen. Did I feel any different? I had to answer a disappointing, nope!

Later, sitting at the kitchen table with breakfast over, I started my third cup of black coffee. That was because my head was still throbbing. So far, I'd been able to hide my discomfort from Ma. But just then, three of my older brothers stomped into the room.

"C'mon, little brother, we've got tickets on the next train to Minneapolis." Lyle was always the loudest.

"Wha-a-a?" stammered I, wishing he would speak more softly.

"Happy birthday, old man Basil," said Clyde. "We're taking you to the big city to celebrate."

Arthur was the oldest, and he just stood there in his quiet and reserved way. I did notice a silly smirk on his face, but he said nothing.

On the way to the train station, we met up with this fella who was red in the face and all out of breath. When he finally got wind, he blurts out, "We're at war! Congress declared war on the Central Powers at three o'clock this morning. Now, we're in it, boys. That rotten Hun, Kaiser Wilhelm had better go hide!"

That had been three days and many beers ago. Then, I was sitting in a smoky dirty troop train heading out of Minneapolis chugging its way east. I wasn't yet sure exactly how it had happened, but there I sat with papers in my pocket telling the whole world that I had "Enlisted in the United States Navy as Lands-man striking for Yeoman, effective April 6, 1917."

I had a lot of help getting plastered. Most guilty were my older brothers, with help from some of their buddies. They were a lot older than me and because they were married and had kids, they said they're too old to serve in the military, but that someone had to hold up the Allaway family honor so they elected me by sending my name in to the recruitment office. Ma and Pa had eleven kids, seven were boys and I just happened to be in the middle. Those after me were still too little, so I guess that's okay 'cause I needed a job anyway.

So why they dragged me all the way from Iowa clear up there to Minneapolis, Minnesota, suddenly became real clear. Happy birthday, indeed!

By the time I flushed my hangover, I was on a train with orders to report to Basic Training, Newport, Rhode Island.

I must have been outa my mind.

So, I wrote all this down just as that smoky dirty troop train headed out of Minneapolis chugging its way to Chicago. And, I was staring at a newspaper headline spread across my lap in the *St. Paul Star* for April 6th reading: **"WAR DECLARED!"** And the subtitle under the headline said, "3-Year Neutrality Ends; Central Powers Now U.S. Enemy." It was a spooky omen that Congress should declare war on Germany and others on the exact day of my birthday. It was scarier still that that's also the same day I signed up. I was going into an unknown war, a new life and I was scared as hell.

This was an especially warm spring day, so a lot of the coach windows were open, but the breeze was not the least bit refreshing as it carried all the sulfur-smelling coal smoke right into the coaches.

I saw my first lady's leg above the ankle that day. That was something that would never happen back in Iowa. Oh, joy! Some very flashy ladies were at the train station when they boarded all us new military types and they sure strutted around on the platform, flashing thighs and waving goodbye to somebody or anybody. I thought maybe that's why the engineer of the train was so slow getting it rolling.

Speaking of rolling, the motion was beginning to make me sick again. My head hurt something awful anyway and the stinky smoke wasn't helping any. I asked a fella with "SP" written on his arm where the club car was and he said, "No booze for you, sailor."

So, there was nothing else to do except snooze, but that didn't last very long. The train was following the old Mississippi right down through Red Wing when I'm suddenly jolted out of sleep by this army type who had his hand in my pocket with a good grip on my wallet. Now, I'm not a big man, but my sudden reaction cut his lip and bloodied his nose pretty good. And as he retreated down the aisle, I patted my inner coat pocket to be sure I still had my billfold, and was reassured by the lump of it.

Well, I'll be switched, if that army idiot didn't show up again ten minutes later in the company of two military policemen. He had them convinced that I had slugged him while stealing his purse, and he wanted me arrested for assault.

His name was Luke Lufkin and he had blood in his eye, figuratively speaking.

"So, it's you again," sneered the guy with the SP armband. "A damned troublemaker, heh?"

I was so shocked by this unexpected development that my brain refused to allow any utterance other than a stammer.

"This is a frame-up," I finally managed to blurt out; "This guy was picking my pocket while I slept."

"Oh, yeah?" says Lufkin. "What'd you do with my billfold?" He then looks at the cop and says, "Frisk him, you'll see!"

Well, I willingly surrendered to the search because I knew he was fibbing, but that was the wrong thing to do. That sneaky thief had stolen mine and planted his own wallet while I slept. What a scam! And I was left defenseless.

You could tell that the copper with the SP armband had already made up his mind and had me already court-martialed, so he wouldn't believe anything I said, anyway.

They already had me in handcuffs, when my salvation arrived in the form of another recruit named Cecil who had been sitting across the aisle.

"Hold on, officer!" he interrupted. "You've got the wrong man! I witnessed the whole affair, and this guy Lufkin is a con artist."

He explained the whole thing in detail to the skeptical shore patrol, who then reluctantly released my handcuffs and put them on Lufkin.

"Now, what about my wallet?" I complained. "He must have it." A thorough search revealed no such, so he must have stashed it somewhere.

"Where is it?" I asked politely.

"Burn in Hell!" was his only reply, as the police escorted him away.

So that's how I lost my billfold and money my first day in the Navy, and made two lifelong enemies. The other was the SP guy, who threw a barb at me over his shoulder as he escorted Lufkin away: "I still think you're a troublemaker, Basil a bitter herb, and I'm going to keep a sharp eye on you. Cross me one more time and it will mean brig time, guilty or not." He mumbled my first name, laughing all the while as he strode away down the aisle. What a pompous ass!

Not all was lost, however, as I met Cecil Martin, who seemed to be an upright and honest guy. I thanked him for getting me out of that pickle. As it happened, he was also going to Newport and we were going to be in the same training camp together.

"Well at least your folks didn't name you Rosemary," Cecil said with a chuckle. And I could not help but see some humor somewhere in the situation. "Or maybe, Dill," he added with a wink.

"Cut the crap," said I, feigning a playful punch at his chin. "From now on just call me Pete. I always admired the strength and power in the hard old face of Simon Peter amongst the statues in church, so from now on just call me Pete."

So it was that Cecil Martin and I turned out to be close and sincere friends.

#

It took two days for that stupid train to get from Minneapolis to Chicago, a mere four hundred and thirty miles. If this were to be any indication of how the war would be fought, the Huns would be calling us the United Snails of America.

They held us over for two more days in Chicago until we could get the right train for Providence. The accommodations weren't half bad; as they put us up in a fancy hotel, and it had a bar! We had been warned to stay sober, but we hadn't seen any sign of "POOPS." (That's the nickname Cecil and I thought up meaning, "**P**etty **O**fficer **O**f **P**olice, **S**tupid.")

I was able to wire my brothers for some money, so we took an unscheduled "liberty" in Chicago. With a whole afternoon to kill, Cecil decided we were going to rent a boat and some gear and go fishing on Lake Michigan.

"I've always wanted to catch one of those big mean old Muskies," he told me. "And, we'll get a big bottle of gin to go along with us to ward off motion sickness."

"How about some ladies?" I asked meekly.

"Plenty of time for that," he scolded. "Remember, we're in the Navy now!" Cecil Martin was one of those roly-poly big guys who are, but never look fat. He was slightly balding but always had a light in his eyes that seem to say "I know what you're thinking, and it's okay." His nose was too small to complement his wide happy smile. The constant grin did little to hide his rotten teeth that looked like old lady Miller's falling-down unpainted picket fence back in Iowa.

So, we went fishing on a windy Great Lake. His two hundred and fifty pounds in the stern almost swamped the little rowboat. His weight raised the bow and my one-hundred-twenty-pound puny self up into the air much of the time. I don't know if I was more airsick or seasick.

The wave motion (or the gin) was really getting to me, when I got the first bite. Setting the hook like my daddy had taught me to do was easy, but then my problems started. I tugged, and reeled, and tugged and reeled until I thought I would reel, when the line suddenly went slack.

Secretly relieved, I reeled in, and landed a… Horrors! Both of us leaned over the gunwale and puked. I had hooked a half-rotten human hand, with some white stringy stuff hanging out of it.

Recovering from this trauma, I cut the line and said, "Let's get out of here."

Cecil said, "Yeah, we'll stop and tell the coppers."

"No way," said I, "let them find their own dead bodies. I've never had any respect for the law, and I'm not about to start now."

Cecil shook his head in disgust.

"You're a real scoundrel!"

"Yeah, I don't deny it!"

Well, the next day we were scheduled to be in Providence, Rhode Island, and then down to the Naval Training Station at Newport. We were on a new train, moving much faster right down through Indiana, Ohio and West Virginia. They had us locked up in two Pullman coaches with our own dining car. At least it was all Navy without any Army types. Yes, old Poops was still along for the ride and he kept watching me like a hawk. I felt that he'd throw me in the brig if I belched and forgot to say, "Pardon me!"

We picked up a newspaper before we left Chicago, and it told us that all of Europe was in an uproar. The Frogs and the Limeys were happy because America had now entered the Great War. But the Huns were defiant, claiming America might be ready to fight, but that we were six to twelve months away from being "fighting ready." Talk among the guys here was that our Navy was nothing but a quiet, sleepy institution where old sailors were passing time waiting for their retirement pensions.[1]

Many of the warships were still powered by old-fashioned boilers, coal fired. Those old-style ships fill up much of their hold with piles and piles of coal, and require a lot of extra manpower to move it. Only a very few of the newest ships were powered by oil. The Navy was so unprepared for that war that scuttlebutt said a lot of shortcuts were going to be made in order to get men and equipment into action in the shortest time possible. Our biggest job was probably going to be helping the British by hauling soldiers over to Europe. They said that we were going to skip over most of the basic training program and we would be in the middle of the war in less than two months.

Cecil and me got a good poker game going with some of the other fellows and took 'em for over $200. Later someone suggested craps, to which we readily agreed, and promptly lost it all.

It was swell being eighteen and really a man out of short pants at long last. The wicked ways of the world's hooch, tobacco and wild women was on a nonstop collision course with my altar-boy Catholic upbringing. My good old Ma was probably praying for me, but if anybody was listening, it certainly wasn't me.

Later, I told Cecil, "I'm new at that game of dice but wait until I learn to cheat, like they did, and we'll get it all back!" You know I really am a scoundrel!

Chapter 2

Texas Mud
September 22, 1942

Dear Putzi:

Well, I didn't get a chance to write you for several days so now I will tell you what happened after that. They started to march us around in the dark but I couldn't keep up on account of my ankle although they had taped it up. So we picked up bedding and they put us in tents. By the time we were in bed it was 3:30 am in the morning and I hardly got to sleep when someone whistled in my ear and says its time to get up which was 5:30 am in the morning.

It was very cold and dark and we had to scrub out our tent which had a floor made out of cement with water from a hose. It was Sunday so after a while we were lined up and marched to breakfast where we had to stand two hours. The trays were greasy and the breakfast was likewise something called shingle, left over from World War 1, but we lived through the day although we spent six hours in mess line and nothing to do except pick up a few snipes around our tent. In the meantime I seemed to have a terrible hangover or something.

The next day was a busy one, believe me. The first thing after breakfast we lined up for shots and I don't mean bourbon although I certainly could of stood one. After that still feeling dopey we were took to a big classroom and gave a long test as to our mental incapacity. Most of it was pretty simple stuff to be giving a bunch of grown up men so I guess I must of passed because the next day they gave me my uniform. After all the tests to see if you fit and where you don't fit, they put all the names in a hat and shake them up and then say, well, this man goes to the infantry and this one to the medicks, etc. So they assign me to the engineers because I have hairy ears although I don't know which end of a shovel is the right one to use against the enemy. Two days later we embark for places unknown under a tough sergeant.

The second evening we had to wait several hours at Pueblo, Colorado and spent it walking up and down the main drag. The said above mentioned sergeant would not permit us to enter any saloon along the way so our tongue was hanging out. But when we got back to the railroad station he got busy talking to a pretty girl and we snook in two at a time and had a beer in the station lunchroom. The next day we spent several hours each in Amarillo, Texas and Lubbock, Texas with like results but no beer at all. Well, at 5:00 am in the morning we arrived at a little country station and were met by trucks and hauled into Camp Berkeley, Texas to join the 456th Engineer Depot Co.

The mud was a foot deep and the hut they put us in was unfinished and unfurnished and full of shavings and dirt. So first we had to swamp it out and get our beds sat up and so forth. We did not finish by breakfast time and we were tired and covered with mud. It being Saturday and inspection day the Captain very kindly excused us from being inspected because we were so muddy and so forth. Hoping you are the same, I remain,

Yours truly, *Gomer Fudd*

P.S. It's been a tough day, and I have memories just like it from that other war, which was Navy instead of Army, remember?

#

Boot Camp
April 20, 1917

Our train had been met at Providence by a chief boatswain's mate, and four busses. We sensed immediately that our comfort and our ease was coming to a fast end; that some unknown fate waited just out of sight around the corner, like a dragon. This old chief was so wrinkled we weren't sure if he had any bones inside his skin at all. He was certainly proof that our Navy was nothing but old sailors waiting to retire. But, his bark was louder than anyone imagined, as the only language he could understand was "Yell-ese."

Some of the men filed off the bus and had begun to mill around, lighting up smokes.

"No smoking!" he bellowed.

Some of us either didn't hear him or had chosen to pretend that we didn't hear him. Then it happened!

One of the first things any sailor learns is how to handle a fire hose, but in this case, we were on the wrong end of the fog spray nozzle. And it certainly got everyone's attention in a big wet hurry. Nobody had to be told twice to extinguish his smokes.

"Fall in!" he barked. "Line up on the sailor with the flag! He's called the guide-on. Hup to it!"

After much cussing and fussing, he finally managed to get us all in some sort of a formation. But that didn't last very long, only until he commanded, "Left face!"

Some of the fellows from rural areas had been so underprivileged that many didn't even know his right foot from his left, and utter chaos followed. I'd never seen such a variety of red skin as that old chief displayed in his neck and face. I'd swear that even his wattle was alive. He looked like a Thanksgiving turkey. He sputtered something unintelligible, but somehow got us loaded into the four battleship gray busses.

"How long does boot camp last, Chief?" called one man after we were all on the bus.

"The rest of your life, rookie!" he yelled back.

A half-hour bus ride later, we got dumped off at a dock and loaded aboard a huge tugboat. The tug chugged across the bay and tied up alongside of an old sailing vessel with a banner proclaiming "Naval Training Station at Newport, Rhode Island." The famous old frigate USS *Constellation* served as the receiving ship, where we were all checked in and given a big sealed envelope full of papers.

Hours later, it seemed we were at a mess hall just inside the main gate at the Newport base. After chow, we were issued a blanket and a large white bag, which somebody said was called a "fart sack."

"Do you sleep inside this thing, or what?" I asked Cecil.

"Dunno," he replied.

It was after 10 PM and I was dog tired, so I just climbed into the bag to sleep. It should have had buttons or a zipper down one side, 'cause it was awful hard to turn around in, because I felt like I was wrapped up in a cocoon.

Well, I had barely gotten to sleep, when the lights flashed on and this most god-awful racket bombarded our ears, jolting us awake with such sudden force that I ripped myself right out of that white bag. I later learned that it was a mattress cover made to protect the three-inch-thick straw mattresses so common in the Navy. No such things as sheets or pillows were allowed.

That red-faced chief wore a cruel smirk on his pink face as he forced a long billy club around and around inside a galvanized corrugated garbage can. It looked like his neck wattle was standing at attention. The racket was unbelievable, to which the chief added his own gruff voice, "Up and at 'em, scum. You go to breakfast in ten minutes!"

"Jeez," I asked Cecil, "what time is it?"

"Three-thirty," he said, "still the middle of the night."

Breakfast was our first introduction to a watery chipped beef in brown gravy slopped on burned toast. Somebody's gotta develop a slang name for that! After breakfast, we were issued more clothes and then returned to the barracks to clean it up.

Some fellows from the rural areas were so backward that many had never had a hot shower or a full suit of clothes or even shoes. Most could not read or sign their name.

By dawn, we were lined up at the infirmary for medical checkups.

Many of us had never been to a doctor or a dentist so the complete physicals they gave us were a scary experience. Those instruments for taking blood pressure or listening to the heart filled these men with dread. Vaccination shots were the worst! When we went by, in single file, the doctor would stick a man in the right arm with a long needle. We had a little patch of iodine there, but the recruit in front of me was so scared that he forgot to move on after getting stuck. So when the doctor turned around for the next man, he stuck the first brown spot that he saw, with the result that the man got a double dose and fainted, falling on the floor, everyone laughing at him. But, I was next and did not feel much like laughing.

Well, that all happened a month before and then, we moved to another secret location, learning close order drill, marching, naval terminology and courtesy. We had to memorize the UCMJ (Uniform Code of Military Justice) and work much from the Navy's "bible" called "The Bluejacket's Manual." I had been appointed to company orderly, because of my typing skills and education level, and as a result, I got out of some of the marching and drills, but still had to attend all classroom work. These guys were too easy. I thought it would be easy to "con" them into believing almost anything!

Remember "Poops," the shore patrol petty officer who gave me so much trouble on the train? Well, one day I was up at the CO's office doing some paperwork, when I thought I heard his squeaky voice. He was walking down the corridor to the head. Outside, he had parked his truck and had come inside to use the toilet. He hadn't seen me, so I followed quietly until I could peek in and see his feet under the stall. The noise he made was gross, and I took full advantage of my opportunity by rolling a lit M-80 "torpedo" firecracker up against the back of the stool where he was sitting.

Ker-blam! The report came, as I was already fifty feet out the back door. The blast was followed by a lot of cursing which I didn't stick around to listen to. Later, it was rumored that an eight-inch hole was blown in the bottom back of the ceramic commode, emptying all the contents onto the floor. We never did hear what might have happened to Poops, but it must have hurt something awful!

The next day, I got a little nervous when our cranky old chief ordered me to report to the lieutenant commander who was in charge of personnel. I imagined that his bobbing Adam's apple was actually smiling

"Do you know why, Chief?" I asked.

"Nope. The order just came down for you to get your butt up there on the double."

"This must be it," I worried as I ran back to the HQ complex. I had hoped that the Poops incident was behind me.

Nervously, I saluted the commander, who then smiled and said, "Sit down, Seaman, and be at ease." You could have knocked me over with a feather.

"You're twenty-one, according to your records," he began. It was a question.

"Yes, sir!" I lied.

"And you've had three years of liberal arts college?"

"Yes, sir!" Another lie. Poops was getting further away from my mind.

"Why don't we have any birth certificate or college transcript?" He was getting suspicious.

"It was a small college housed in unused rooms of the county courthouse in Strawberry Point, Iowa," I answered, "and four months ago, a fire burned the building to the ground and all records were lost." At least, the last part was true.

The answer seemed to satisfy him and he said, "We're desperate for leaders, and there's a place waiting for you at Annapolis, in the Officer's Candidate School, if you want it."

Now, I had fully considered this possibility already, and had decided weeks earlier that I wanted no part of being a "shave-tail" ensign or lieutenant..

"No, sir!" I replied without hesitation.

"Well, you are plenty qualified for leadership," he stammered. "We're desperate for leaders, so help me out, here."

After a few moments of silence, he added, "If you're striking for yeoman then, I'm going to recommend that we start you off as second-class petty officer, effective next month when you finish basic training... Dismissed!"

And that was it! I saluted smartly, did an about-face and never saw the man again.

"My gosh," I said aloud, as I walked back to our barracks, "I've just been bumped up four whole grades, from E-1 to E-5." I felt on top of the world, but then, I realized that it was a world at war, and nothing was permanent.

Anyway, I could hardly wait to find my best friend, Cecil, and share my good news.

#

Happy birthday, Uncle Sam! We graduated just for you, that day on July the 4th.

Most of our company had been given two white stripes designating a rate of seaman apprentice. Glancing around after our grand review parade, I noticed several full seaman ratings with three white stripes. But a half-dozen of us got to wear red chevrons with the rating eagle of petty officer. The Navy was so desperate for leaders to build up a fighting force, that men with any skills or education were instantly promoted. A few of our guys had college credits and had already departed for Officer's Candidate School.

It had been said that any recruit with a high school or higher education was immediately groomed for leadership or positions of responsibility, and I guess that it was true. I'm sure glad that I had a decent education. How that happened was kind of funny. To hear Ma tell it, she was a dyed-in-the-wool Methodist, but the only town my Pa could find decent work in didn't have any public school. The Catholics ran the only school in the area, but Pa couldn't afford to pay them. So, according to Ma, she struck a deal with the head priest that if she and the whole family converted to the Catholic faith, then he'd allow all her kids to attend his school.

I was scheduled a week later to go to a yeoman's mate special school to learn more about Navy records, reports and payroll bookkeeping. It would last for two months, and then I assumed that I would be posted to a ship.

A lot happened that month. My friend Cecil Martin also got a rating; he was now a quartermaster's mate third class, and he was really innovative when it came to scrounging illegal (or unofficial) supplies. We were not allowed off base at all that month, but somehow he managed to get hold of some contraband to help slake everybody's thirst.

Barracks 12, the one that was next to ours, made a deal to collaborate with some of our guys to smuggle in several cases of beer, and Cecil was right in the middle of it. Well, to make a long story short, one night old Poops came snooping around over there, and everyone in Barracks 12 got put on report, and given extra duty.

We waited for the axe to fall, but it never did for us. It was reported that Poops was limping pretty bad and using a cane. Someone said they saw him standing outside our barracks the next night, looking puzzled and just scratching his head...?

I wasn't sure, but I thought the axe did fall on Cecil, as his name showed up on the "mess-cooking" assignment list the following morning. It could have been by chance, but nobody thought so. Mess cooks in the Navy don't usually do any cooking, instead they "help out" by scrubbing out garbage cans, peeling spuds, or washing dishes. The name is misleading, just like in the Army where KP stands for kitchen police, and they sure as heck don't guard the kitchen.

Cecil had been assigned down there for two weeks, and I visited him a couple of times. He had been stuck in the dirtiest, most vile job they had, called scullery. All day long, he emptied smelly flyblown garbage cans and then scrubbed them out with hot water and disinfectant. The smell was so bad that the "garbage control house" where he worked, was located in a field, almost one hundred yards away from the mess hall. One day, while holding my nose, I asked him why he poured kerosene into the cans before scrubbing them.

"Take a look-see," he said, pointing to a dirty but just emptied can. "It's a cheap and effective insecticide."

I obliged and took a look, promptly vomiting. The can was crawling with millions of white, slimy maggots.

Cecil returned to our barracks two weeks later. But he still wouldn't tell me how he managed to get off base and smuggle all that beer in. Must have been a "trade secret" that he wanted to keep quiet for possible future use.

We read in a current newspaper that the first American troops ("Doughboys") arrived in France on June 28, 1917. They were called the American Expeditionary Forces (AEF).

You know that we Americans invented the "convoy" system, which was originally opposed by the British. Before destroyers escorted the supply convoys, one out of every four ships leaving Britain was sunk by German U-boats.[2]

As we got closer to completion of basic training, we found we had more time to sit around the barracks and "shoot the bull." Sailors always like to joke about the other branches of military service. We knew that the marines and doughboys always considered us no higher than "swabbies" of the deck, and their newspaper cartoons never pictured one of us without somebody holding a mop and mop bucket. So, just to set the record straight, we had a symbol to use in picturing them… either a paring knife used to peel potatoes, or a shovel for digging latrines and foxholes. We might have to peel a few spuds, but dig a latrine? …Never!

Speaking of Marines, you know that they are really nothing but a branch of the Navy, anyway.

One morning, the mess hall posted a rare sign, a menu, politely informing us what we would be having for dinner. This had never happened before, so everybody became quite suspicious. The notice said, "Liberty Cabbage for dinner tonight, Bring your best appetites."

Well, as you can imagine, this riddle was the talk of the day, with many guesses as to what "Liberty Cabbage" might be. None of the cooks down at the galley were of any help. They just smiled a smug secret smile and shook their heads. "Wait until dinner, you'll see!" Some of the fellows got a pool going to bet money on the winning guess.

Tension built all afternoon, until finally the camp bugler announced, "Mess call."

The mystery was quickly solved, when it became known that German-Americans, always under suspicion, had changed the name of sauerkraut to "liberty cabbage." One guy named Schwarzwalder was the only one to guess the riddle and win the pool. Then someone else got up a pool to guess what nationality Schwarzwalder was…?

Before leaving for yeoman school, I made contact with some incoming recruit to dispose of my contraband supply of booze and cigarettes. During the first two weeks of basic boot, we weren't allowed to go to the PX or anywhere else on or off base, and some of these stashed "essentials" would be of invaluable worth to some enterprising newcomer. I remember wishing that I could have taken some of that stash with me, but could only hope to convert some of it to ready cash.

As a parting shot, that old red-faced chief, the one that looked like a turkey, called me in to his office that last day to say thanks. He was shaking so severely I thought his Adam's apple and neck wattle appeared to be at war with each other.

"What for?" I asked.

"The new breed of punks like you," he replied, "give me clear conscience to retire. Now, get outa here before I decide to give you what you really deserve. Because if I did, I'd have to re-enlist just to be a witness at your court-martial."

Chapter 3

The Kiyi Brush
October 19, 1942

Dear Putzi:

I haven't had a chance to write before this because of the heavy duties of a Private in this war. We have had about six hours of drill and two of school each day and I am learning fast in spite of my age and the stiffness of my bones. Of the 25 of us which came down from Utah, 19 are over forty physically and 2 of us are over twelve mentally. The Lieutenant says that he had heard that nowadays they just felt of a guy and if he was warm they said you are in the Army but he didn't believe it until he seen us. Some of this gang are real characters. One of them is tall and skinny with a pinhead and the Sergeant says that it takes so long for a brain wave to reach his feet that he will never learn to keep step. All he does at night is sit in a corner and play a mouth organ and eat ice cream.

Another guy is rolley fat and short and always causes us bad points at inspection time because he never takes a bath and his bunk is so messed up that he smells bad. Our kind old Sergeant had a word about him too and we learned about kiyi scrub brushes on bare skin in a cold shower. The rolley fat guy turned red all over, but he still smells bad.

There is no beer here in this camp. The nearest town is Abilene and there is also no beer because this is the dry part of Texas but bootleg whiskey for $8 dollars a pint.

Well, yesterday I got quite a kick. The Captain he called me over so I went into his office and saluted and he said, "That is the wrong way to salute, try again."

So I tried for eight times and he finally told me. "That will do for the time being and sit down."

Then he asked me, "Are you the man who was in the Navy in the last World War?"

And I said, "Yes sir."

So he asked me what I was doing in the Army. So I told him about the President and my neighbors but he didn't let me finish.

Then he said, "Did you ever consider applying for the O.C.S.?"

And I said, "What is that sir?"

And he said it was the officer candidate school.

I said, "No sir that I am too old to be a shavetail."

So he looked at me kinda funny like and said, "Oh no, there are lots of branches where you could qualify which would perhaps be more suitable than the engineers."

So I told him I would think it over and then I left.

So last night I thought it over and I remembered the last world war #1 and two of my buddies who got commissions in September, 1918. One of them was dematerialized in November after he had spent $500 dollars for uniforms. The other guy didn't get out for three years.

So I decided that I would not like to be a Second Lieutenant but if they would offer to make me a Colonel I might consider it or a Master Sergeant.

So this morning I told the Captain and he said, "Very well."

Then when I was about to leave he said to me that I would be excused from ordinary drill and on Monday I would report to him. He said as long as I didn't want to be a shavetail 2ⁿᵈ Lieutenant he would make me the office runner and assistant mail orderly but I would not be exempt from hikes and special drills such as rifle and gas.

I could of gone to Abilene this afternoon but decided to stay in camp. Some of the boys are now coming back and so I must quit as they are pretty drunk and noisy. Hoping you are the same, I remain   Yours truly, *Gomer Fudd*

P.S. I swear this war is... what's that French word? *De'ja vu* all over again. Here's what I mean:

#

26

Yeoman School
August 27, 1917

Yeoman school was a real featherbed. We were up in New Jersey, and we had liberty almost any night we wanted. It had gotten to the point where I'd rather stay in the barracks than go out drinking with the boys every night and suffering the resulting hangover. It was a lot more fun to go to New York City sightseeing.

There were too many students there for the few required duty watches. A Marine base next door provided most of the security and police patrol duties. Only once in two weeks did any of us draw guard duty and mine was usually to belt on a forty-five semi-automatic pistol and march around the mess hall for four hours to keep any would-be scavengers out. It was a big farce because I had made friends with some of the chief cooks who worked the night shift so I was the biggest scavenger of all, getting almost any snack my hungry tummy required. If I had this duty more often, I'd have gotten fat for sure.

One night when I had the duty, the officer of the day came sneaking around trying to test whether or not his guards were awake. Sleeping on guard duty was a capital offense, so we had been warned not to get caught. Well, this young green ensign thought he was going to advance his career by catching somebody asleep at their post, and he came a sneaking around one moonless night about 03:30 hours.

He didn't see me hidden in the shadows between two buildings, and I let him creep up to within ten feet, when I hollered in my loudest voice, "Halt, Who goes there? Identify yourself, or I'll shoot!" I swear, the poor bastard must have peed his pants. That was before he jumped backward, tripped over a cement block and fell headfirst into one of those maggot-filled garbage cans. And that was the last time we ever had any smart-alec junior officers intruding into our sleep time.

One Friday night we went to a Navy Club dance, and I began to see why God in His wisdom, made women. Oh, joy! We had been forced to be hermits for so long, I almost forgot that pretty girls even existed. There were some real beauties there, and at a nickel a dance, I soon ran out of spending money.

Those girls sure took a tumble over a uniform, and one in particular, named Pearl something or other, liked me so much that I got the last five dances for free. She was seventeen and a real princess. Joyful! Joyful! Friday then became a day of anticipation, one full of hope and full of fear all at the same time; hope to see her again, and fear that she would not be at the next week's dance. What a dunce I had been to not get her full name or address.

Our yeoman's mate school was in Hoboken, just across the Hudson River from Manhattan and New York City. When we first arrived, we were told that the next class would not start for another three weeks. So, in the meanwhile, all fifty of us would be assigned to such things as policing the grounds (Picking up cigarette "snipes"), or raking, or sweeping and mopping ("compartment cleaning"), or mess cooking ("scullery").

It was most odd to look around this motley bunch of candidates at morning muster and see that everyone had the chevron of a petty officer, some third class and a few second class, and then ponder the situation. Not one of these men had been in the service four months before, and here they all stood with stripes of leadership, but all still expected to do the work of a rookie boot. I couldn't see how they could all be liars and con men, like me.

We understood that in the pre-war Navy this much advancement in rate and pay grade would normally take almost ten years! Like I said earlier, there we were, sitting on top of the world, but beware, the world was ready to crack into a thousand splinters.

Anyway, there we stood at morning muster, everybody at rigid attention, while the bugle sounded morning colors, and as the flag of this great nation slid up the flagpole, all respect was rendered with a smart salute.

"Two!" snapped the master at arms, as the last tones of the bugle faded. All saluting arms snapped back down, in one accord, with thumbs properly lined up on the trouser seam.

"Parade rest!" ordered the MAA. "Now hear this…" And he droned on, naming names and assignments to various work details. Some were assigned to be "captains of the head," scrubbing showers and toilets.

After naming just about everybody, he continued, "Now, according to BuNav, all you second class petty officers were eligible for Officer's Candidate School, but turned it down…" He was talking to only six of us. "…So, we're going to have a little contest: How many of you can type at forty words per minute?"

All six of us raised our hands.

"Fifty words…?"

Four hands stayed raised up.

"Sixty words…?"

Still four.

"How many of you have ever type-cut the new mimeograph stencils?"

My hand and one other remained in the air.

"Good," exclaimed the MAA. "You two report to Lieutenant Househoder over in the Ad Building. You'll be working for him until your class starts."

I was beginning to wonder whether or not this "con" had any payoff, but when the other four unlucky typists were assigned to repaint the supply building, I knew I had made the right choice. Almost everybody in the Navy had to learn the most efficient way to wield a paintbrush, at some time during their career; but not me on that day!

Well, as it turned out, we two lucked out with the most posh jobs of all, typing up lesson plans, which we duplicated and stockpiled on a shelf, which would later be handed out to us and others in class. By the time it came around for classroom examinations, or pop quizzes, we would already know all the answers!

The other guy working with me was named Buford, a real fruitcake. He was such a "perfect mama's boy" that we didn't get along at all. Too bad for him if he gets assigned the same ship as me, because he'd drive me nuts and I'd probably throw the priss overboard some dark and stormy night.

Soon however, I no longer had to worry about interaction with that jerk, because he got delayed and was to be assigned to a different class, probably the next one after me. I learned something: When you're very very good at something, don't let anybody know, or you'll get stuck doing the same job forever.

I had been in class now for four weeks, and that poor sap Buford was still cutting stencils. It was hard to tell whether he was just too stupid to know the difference, or if he really planned it that way. If it meant anything, he'd have the whole course memorized by the time he started school. I didn't do badly myself, and was holding top of my class with ease.

The record keeping that yeomen perform covers all facets of personnel control. We were responsible for the upkeep of enlistment records, advancement, payroll, discharge, transfers and all the required paperwork to keep the naval bureaucracy flowing smoothly.

Yeoman school was going by too fast and with only four weeks remaining, Pearl failed to show up at the Friday dance. That was a terrible blow, leaving me with only three more chances to see her again, not nearly enough time. Oh, woe was me! Maybe Buford had the right idea after all.

#

But, I worried in vain. Oh, joy! I was in love! The next two weeks passed by me while I was in a fog. Accounting journals and ledgers, payroll vouchers and typing ribbons all now merged with more important things. Things like roses, candy, personal grooming, Wildroot Crème Oil, colognes and "foo-foo" dust.

There was this new dance that somebody down in South Carolina invented, called the Charleston. Oh! did my gal like to shimmy! I've always had three clumsy left feet and never learned any of the so-called "social graces" in high school, and had always been shy. When I first met Pearl, she sort of smiled when I tried dancing and said, "Let me show you how to do it, handsome!…" Ever since then, I let her "lead" me down the primrose path. I was still kind of backward, but was learning to shimmy too.

Pearl had really spiced up my life, like when the top two buttons were left open on her amply filled up blouse. The jiggle of her soft chest drove me nuts! I was too bashful to tell you any more of the really good things about her, and would certainly be ashamed to write any of them all down on a piece of paper. Oh, joy!

When I was on the base, and supposed to be listening to lectures or following some lesson plan, I'd often daydream a lot instead and doodle nonsense things like:

Our love, my turtle dove, is ever warm…
Your sighs, my dear, are like a tropic storm…
A playful kiss could set the woods on fire,
And make my lovesick heart a burning pyre.

It was a good thing that I learned all those lessons in advance, by typing all those stencils. I was still at the top of my class and had been told that when yeoman's mate school finished on September 27th, my new billet was the Brooklyn Navy Yard where I was scheduled to get a ship. There were two possible choices waiting in dry dock, but they wouldn't tell me which one.

Just up from the Portsmouth Navy yard was the seized German raider, the *Prinz Eitel Friedrich*. She had been very active in surprise attacks on Allied shipping early in the war, and last year, she ran into Norfolk to escape being captured by a British destroyer. She was a famous converted liner that was being outfitted for troop transportation to France.

I was never a brave person and would just be glad to be assigned to a transport instead of a fighting war ship.

The other ship I could be assigned to was also a famous converted liner, the *Friedrich der Grosse*, which was Germany's first liner to exceed ten thousand tons, launched in 1896, and she had almost completed her conversion to transporting troops. They planned to rename her the U.S.S. *Huron*.

Lieutenant Househoder called me up to his office just ten days before school was over. I sat in the outer office waiting for him for over an hour, and who was there, still diligently typing mimeograph stencils?

"Buford," I said, "you'll never get out of here, unless you start screwing up by making more mistakes."

He grunted something unintelligible, and kept on sweating.

Just then the inner office door burst open and a seaman was hustled out, escorted by two strong-arm shore patrol coppers.

"Allaway, front and center!" growled the lieutenant. "And secure the hatch."

I hesitated for a second until Buford snickered, "He means get your butt in there and close the door after you."

A cold chill ran up my spine as I rendered the required respect of a smart hand-salute.

"Forget that!" he said. "Sit down. Can I call you Pete?"

He had a wicked sinister gleam in his eye. Bells went off in my head warning me that something was horribly wrong.

"If you like, sir." I hesitated while finding a seat. "The seaman just arrested….?"

"Caught stealing," interrupted the lieutenant. "Too stupid… No imagination…"

His words hung on the stagnant air like a hangman's noose, while his piercing eyes searched for some unknown thing in the depth of my soul.

After a somewhat pregnant pause, I simply asked, "You wanted to see me, sir?"

The air thickened.

"Yes, Pete," he said. "Would you like to make some extra money?"

And the conversation went on; it was an illegal payroll scheme for which he needed a discreet accomplice and would have got us each an extra grand. He told me not to say no, because he knew who it was that blew up the commode back in Newport, Rhode Island, and sent a shore patrolman to the hospital, and if I didn't go along with his scheme, he'd have me court-martialed. So began my "career."

He said he chose me for this job because of my education and because I'd be shipping out in ten days so nobody could ask me anything that might trip us up.

I wondered if my con career was catching up to me? After finishing the details, his dismissal was curt and my limbs felt slow and heavy as I trudged through the outer office, imagining a ball and chain already attached to my leg.

He did tell me, however, that I was being assigned to the *Huron*, and she would be ready to sail in less than a month.

Of interest to all sailors, I learned *Huron* was built at "Vulcan" Stettin by Hamburg-American, was 10,696 gross tons displacement, 546 feet in length with a 60-foot beam. She was fitted with coal-powered quadruple expansion engines powering two screws capable of 14.5 knots speed. Her full complement would be about 440 men, and I would be one of them! It was scary to think about. In addition to our complement, we would be cramming more than 5,000 soldiers into spaces designed for 2,300 passengers.

I had nightmares that night, like fighting off fiery devils with a wet swab. Finally my wet mop doused their hell fires, and I got a little rest. All the while, I thought Lucifer was laughing in the background. I wanted to get up and go tell Lieutenant Househoder that his deal was off, but I couldn't. Then, I was swimming in burning fuel oil and drowning inside a black cave with over five thousand other floundering men. I had difficulty staying on the surface because a ball and chain kept dragging me under water. Then I woke up, screaming and drenched with sweat.

Chapter 4

Serious Sexy Diseases
October 25, 1942

Dear Putzi:

When the Captain told me I would be exempt from ordinary drill I was very happy but oh how I have changed. Every other day we have a hike or a special drill. The first hike wasn't so bad but the second one we went 28 miles and I sure had blisters not to mention aching mussels. The country was very drab around here and they say that you can look further and see less in Texas than anywhere else and more rivers and less water. Also there are more cows and less milk. We saw some cotton fields, armodillas, possoms, and rattlersnakes all dead which had been run over by a truck I guess.

Today we had what they call extended order drill with rifles which we advance in loose formation at double time against the enemy and when the Sergeant gives the signal we half to flop and roll over behind some cover if possible. That is all very well and good but I wish some general would figure out how to flop and roll over in Texas without getting full of sand burrs and cactis. Them burrs are the meanest thing as back home we called them goats heads. When you try to pick them off they stick to your fingers and I mean bloody stick.

Also we have lectures which we half to attend. One rosy young Lieutenant gave us a lecture about sexy deceases and every time he came to an important part he would blush and then we all had to laugh but he got mad and said it was a serious subject and no laughing matter.

We also had a lecture on maps and the Lieutenant tried to tell us that the V's on the map point upstream so yours truly said that was a funny map and then he got mad too. A little later he started to talk about something else and looked right straight at me and said, "We don't want any comments from the wise guy either."

Last Saturday a few of us went to Abilene but we got disgusted and thought we would half to have our right arm in a sling from saluting so many 2nd Lieutenants. Then we hired a car and went to Albany about 50 miles away where they were wet and have beer and then to Breckenridge where they also do and besides they have a good dance. The car was from a travel agency so we had to take a bust back and when we were waiting at the bust station a MP came up to me and said, "Don't try to take any beer back to camp."

So I said, "No sir," but I had three quarts in a box under my arm which nobody looked into and we got back safely to our hutment and drunk the beer although we had already had too much. The next day I was glad it was Sunday because I sure felt lousy. Hope you are the same,

Yours truly, *Gomer Fudd*

P.S. These officers must consider me to be pretty stupid; nothin' like in the last war. Sometimes I feel like I've been reincarnated from being another person in another time:

#

U.S.S. Huron
October 8, 1917

It took ten days for me to shake all the ghosts out of my conscience, and then we were in barracks at the Brooklyn Navy Yard. We had all day to look over the beautiful *Huron*, sitting high and dry and gleaming with fresh paint in the dry dock. I took pictures fore and aft.

Friedrich der Grosse getting refurbished in Brooklyn dry dock, 1917

My younger brother, Hillary, had sent me a gift. It was one of those new-finagled Kodak cameras that used the smallest size film they could make. It was 616 size and took some really super pictures. It was beyond the capacity of my poor brain to figure out how such a thing could work.

We would be boarding and launching her out the next day. The painters still had to put on her new name. I thought that there would be a re-commissioning ceremony scheduled for sometime later in the week. We were working aboard, but still sleeping in the barracks for a few days.

Friedrich der Grosse getting refurbished in the Brooklyn dry dock, 1917

Some wartime drills had already been started. Everybody had been assigned "battle stations" and mine was second loader on the starboard side six-inch gun, aft. We had six such cannon, three on the port side and three on the starboard. All the other spare deck space had been covered with huge life rafts stacked four, sometimes five deep. She was equipped with thirty-two regular lifeboats but that wouldn't be nearly enough for all the extra doughboys we'd be hauling over to France. At any thought or suggestion of enemy action I had instant recall of my flailing drowning nightmares.

That week would probably be our last chance to take any liberty or shore leave for a while. And the fickle finger of fate had decreed that Pearl was up in Flushing for three or four days visiting a sick aunt. Flushing was too far to travel to on our short liberties.

All my new shipmates could think or talk about was either booze or ladies. Now, I was certainly not against the former, but I had a secret that they don't know about. As far as the latter was concerned, I was too much infatuated with Pearl to even think about other ladies. So, for my time off base, I thought more about a third option: food!

So it was with this in mind that one of the ship's cooks had approached me with an idea.

"We'll be going to sea soon," he began, "and there's a real shortage of fresh fruits and vegetables aboard ship. Now I hear you is from Iowa, so you should know about good ripe corn…?" It was a question.

"Yeah," stammered I, getting the gist of his thought. "There's that big cornfield a mile down Sands Street."

"And the livery stable just outside the gate, where they rent wagons." He winked his eye.

"Is there a moon tonight?" I asked

"Nope."

"Let's meet outside the gate at nine. Bring three mess cooks," I said.

Now, stealing this farmer's corn was simple. It's when a logistical mind can plan an efficient process that success can be almost guaranteed. That is, if you don't get caught. The back road behind the cornfield was wide enough to drive the wagon, pulled by one horse. One man was to walk behind the slow-moving wagon, catching whatever loot those walking in the field threw out to him. Each man in the cornfield would strip two rows; so in short order the wagon would be filled with ripe late September golden cobs of corn. At the end of the front row, the farmer had also planted some choice watermelons, which came flying up to the catcher with unexpected force, shattering several before he got the idea. It was about that time that the old horse got ticked off because we weren't sharing any fresh corn, so he bellowed a loud neigh, which alerted the farmer and resulted in one of our guys taking a little buckshot in the butt.

Well, we got clean away, but now had the problem of getting the corn (and a few melons) in through the base gate.

"Not to worry," said I, producing a stack of gunnysacks from under the buckboard. Once we got the corn bagged, we drove around behind the base to a secluded spot and pitched the bags over the barbed wire fence. The melons, however, did not survive that maneuver. A work detail from the ship would recover the loot in the morning and bribing the sentry on the dock was a simple cinch.

The only evidence we left behind from this little caper was the poor horse. After we got away from the cornfield, we fed him as much green fresh corn as he could eat before returning horse and wagon to the livery stable. Now, green fresh corn causes terrible gas in horses and it took about two hours for this eruption to occur in the poor horse. By the time the livery stable guy started cussing us out we were all sound asleep in our berths.

Pearl was such a different kind of a girl; I was going to hate taking the chance of leaving her there alone with all those military types moving in and out of New York City. I thought that I needed to see her soon and make her promise to quit working at the service organization dances.

#

Whatever crew was still quartered landside, came aboard the next day and stowed all their gear. Our yeoman's office was on the main deck just above the main galley.

The "Charley Noble" and exhaust ducts from the galley below ran up the other side of the bulkhead that my desk faced; and the food preparation smells drove me crazy.

There were four of us sharing the three rooms that served as our office. They were Chief Yeoman Turner, two seaman second-class strikers and myself. The chief and I shared a small adjoining bunkroom. The two strikers were part of the deck crew and had to bunk below. Our boss was Lieutenant (JG) McHenry.

Sailors carried their own hammocks plus seabag, so I took the head and foot lacing off my hammock, and stowed them in my locker. I spread the hammock over the bunk springs. On that went the mattress, covered by a "fart sack" then strapped down by wide, webbed straps to keep them from sliding off in rough weather. On them we placed our blankets. Pillows were unknown.

The painters put on her new name that day, the U.S.S. *Huron*, on both sides of the bow and across the stern fantail. When most of the crew was aboard, the dock was flooded and she floated up from her keel blocks and we were towed to the wet basin for finishing up and to load coal and stores. We already had fresh corn in the cooler. Even the striking yeomen, cooks and quartermasters had to take their shift at shoveling coal into the bunkers, a nasty job which would last for four days.

Staterooms on this ex-luxury liner, that used to accommodate two people, were cut up so badly with temporary berths that the same space would now sleep sixteen, in fold-down bunks arranged four deep. The doughboys and marines we hauled would mess in the plush dining salons, while the crew were assigned separate messes, depending on their watch, just like on any warship. We would seldom have any contact with the troops we would be carrying, and were already grousing about the posh accommodations that they were going to get.

The Brooklyn Navy Yard gate opened out onto Sands Street, and when liberty started at sixteen hundred hours, who should be standing outside the gate waiting for me, but Pearl. She was a lovely lady and a lot of fun, but was beginning to seem a little anxious about a permanent relationship.

That night we went to a movie house to see a funny film starring Mary Pickford and Charlie Chaplin, then to a dinner club. Pearl wanted to stay late and dance, but I was getting a funny feeling about her and made up an excuse.

"Sorry, darling," I lied, "but I've got to get back aboard, as I've got tonight's mid-watch."

I didn't feel any pangs of conscience as I escorted her to her streetcar. Her lingering kiss was evidence of her disappointment. "You'll be sailing in a few days," she said pleadingly. "Will I get to see you before you leave?" She had been pressing against me in the most intimate and provocative manner.

Truthful, this time, I answered, "Probably not, as I've got over four hundred crew members' personnel records and orders to process and file."

Early the next morning, the whole ship was rousted out by the bosun's pipe.

"Now hear this…" sputtered the speakers, "Coaling operations are temporarily suspended, all hands make ready to sail." I could already feel the vibrations from engine room No. 2, which was located two decks below, immediately under the galley.

"What's up?" I asked Chief Turner.

"Two days of sea trials to check this old tub out," he replied. "We'll return afterwards and finish taking on coal and supplies. We're scheduled for our first load of soldiers on Tuesday." Then he added, "Guess I forget to tell you, last night."

I didn't have any assigned departure duties, so wandered down to the P.O. mess deck for some chow.

"No breakfast until we're out of the harbor," announced the mess cook.

Back in the office, I decided to start on my mountain of paperwork. But the noise and clatter of getting under way soon became unbearable.

Outside our office, there was a small, clean area from the break of the forecastle to number-two stack between two three-inch waist guns. From here aft, the deck on each side afforded only a twisting footpath among the maze of gear. Men shouted orders above the shrill whine of the blowers building up pressure in the fire rooms. As we got underway, engineers prowled the deck over the fire rooms, with Stilson wrenches, and their eyes watching the stacks. If there was even a trace of smoke they warned the black gang by banging on the steel vents with the wrenches.

The racket was too much for us to be able to concentrate, so we simply lined the rail and watched the New York skyline and the Statue of Liberty drift by. And as more steam built up, the bridge telegraphed down asking for more revolutions. So the fires increased, and the shrill whine of the blowers on deck became even more obnoxious.

"Hope it's not always like this," I said to the chief, "or the Hun submarines will hear us coming from twenty miles away!"

He assured me that conditions in a war zone would be different.

By then, we were cruising at 14.5 knots, our standard service speed, and things began to quiet down, so we could get back to work. About an hour later, I got some help when the bosun released our two strikers from deck duty, and I set them both to work. Mick Fulleton was an Irisher from Detroit and was small and a little chubby, but he could type almost as fast as I could. The other striker was a tall, lanky Texan called Jefferson Jones, and when the two of them stood side by side, it was easy to see why we quickly nicknamed them "Mutt and Jeff."

Our first day at sea had been interrupted every hour or so with various drills, "fire," gunnery, "collision" and a bunch of other nonsense. The gunnery drill was the only one that I had to go to, but they held it four different times, until my back seemed to break from loading those monster six-inch artillery shells.

I thought that some of that Navy nomenclature was pretty salty, but we heard some new ones that I had to write down:

Beef hearts: Beans, with a rhyming pun on farts.

Binnacle List: A ship's sickbay list.

Blue unction: Blue ointment used to exterminate "crabs."

Buckshee: Surplus, free, anything obtained easy but unexpected.

Bumf: Toilet paper or routine redundant orders.

Charlie Noble: The galley smokestack.

Devil-dodger: Scripture reader or chaplain.

Five by five: Naval bumf. (As opposed to army bumf which is called "Six by four.")

Pung: A sly sleep while on telephone talker duty.

Short arm inspection: Checking penises for signs of venereal disease.

Stanchion: An upright bar, beam, or post used as a support column, usually brass.

There were a lot more, I'll tell you about later. It seems we learned a new word every day.

The chief shared a newspaper from a couple of days earlier about some of our marines that had landed in Belgium. US Marines were fighting so fierce that the Germans had nicknamed them "Devil Dogs." When I read this, I recalled that only a few weeks ago, the Huns were saying that the United States would not be ready to fight effectively for many months. Ha! I thumbed my nose at Germany and the Central Powers!

Another article that affected us said that: "Safely transporting the AEF to France was the Navy's major accomplishment. Rear Admiral Hilary P. Jones commands the newly created Transport Force using a fleet of German merchantmen and passenger liners that had been interned in American ports. Fourteen of them exceeded ten thousand tons each and have become the backbone of the Transport Force, plying between Hampton Roads, New York or Hoboken NJ and Brest or St. Nazaire." I guess that meant us! Go sic 'em, *Huron!*

Chapter 5

Down Under
January 9, 1943

Dear Putzi:

It is a long time since I wrote but here I am in a new joint—Camp Anza, California. It is near to Riverside and the oranges are growing all around here with a sweet blossum smell that would make a skunk throw up. It is a long story about how I come to be here.

First of all furloughs were canceled and those who where gone were recalled back to camp. Then we had intense drills in gas chambers and obstacle courses.

About that time I had to have my teeth fixed so the dentist told me that I didn't have enough good uppers to fix a bridge to, so he would say the best bet would be to have a nice GI plate.

On Thanksgiving day we had a very swell dinner planned but in the morning I was called to the dental clinic and they pulled several teeth and was I mad because the dang dentist didn't spend the holiday with his family. But I managed to plough through the turkey and stuff in spite of a little blood on everything.

Well, I will skip over all the time since then except during Christmas week I was very busy handling the mail and I got quite a bit myself. By then I had no teeth at all on the top but I managed to get enough to eat with soup, ice cream, milk and other condoments.

Last Saturday night was January 2nd we all felt that it was our last night in Camp Barkely because we had been issued all kinds of queer things for tropic use and none of the picked men were allowed to leave camp. However through some magic or otherwise it seemed that the camp was full of whisky which we all indulged.

I had to see the dentist at 6:00 pm in the evening and he told me to come back at 9 so at 9:00 pm in the evening I was drunk when he fitted me with my upper plate which made me look like a horse who has nothing to laugh about and I called him buddy and he was a Captain I guess or maybe a Major. So the next day we still had a drink or two around the place but I can't get used to my face in the mirror.

Well, on Monday night we were given our traveling orders and had several hours to spend before we took the train. We are the headquarters platoon and the rest of the guys stay here and that night they were all or mostly in town. So we took there bunks and placed them on the roof of the hutments.

I shure hope we don't meet them someplace overseas or anyplace because vengeance is sweet. So we got on a train about 9:00 pm in the evening and took off for parts unknown which turned out to be this joint. This is a small place but is full of men who are alerted for overseas. And boy oh boy, we have beer and do we make use of it.

The PX opens at 5:00 pm in the evening and most of us miss our chow so we won't miss any beer. The PX is a big joint filled with mess tables and benches and after a while drunks. We start with a case and after a few bottles to oil things up we start to sing the Engineer's song and Ringadangadoo and other popular numbers. Soon we have an admiring crowd of medicks around who join in the chorus and buy a few more cases to keep the pot aboiling.

A lot of young girls work in the PX which also sells some other stuff and they are receiving a good education in what every young girl should know I guess. They do not permit us to take any beer out but we do so anyhow.

One night we threw a big party in our barracks with the athaletic fund and we all had a good time. We even had a case of coke for the few who didn't like beer but not many.

This country is all full of oranges and stuff around here and is quite pretty but you can't pick any. There are lemons and grape fruits and lots of palm trees with sweet dates not the girl kind. It is hot in the days and cold at night. I went to Lost Angeles with some other fellas but we just wandered around.

You half to stand in line even for a cup of coffee and the surface men were sleeping all over the bust depot on the floor. So it was the only night I was sober and I felt disgusted.

I suppose we will be on a ship pretty soon. We have had a few drills such as gas and climbing landing nets and the senser won't allow us to tell about a few lectures we've had on things that are unmentionable. Hoping you are the same,

Yours truly, *Gomer Fudd*

#

February 24, 1943

Dear Putzi:

From now on I half to be careful what I say on account that the Japs might open my letter and some of them can read English I understand. The Captain said he guessed it would be alright to tell where we had been because everybody knew that anyhow but not to say where we are going which is kinda silly because I don't even know where.

Well, anyhow we are still aboard of a big fast ship which is very crowded with soldiers and nurses. It has been an interesting trip as it is the first time I crossed the Pacific ocean although I crossed the Atlantic ocean thirty times in the last world war #1 when I was in the Navy. So I am an old sailor and never miss a meal which we get only twice per day but some of the boys never get out of there bunks.

And now I am a shellback too having crossed the equator. The whether has been nice most of the time. Onced or twice we thought we were running into a tycoon but they was only little squabbles.

Well, we stopped at Wellington in New Zealand. We didn't have any shore leave exactly but twice we were marched around in rout step and allowed to fall out and rest for an hour or so. We talked to some nice people that gave us a bottle of beer but most of the boys raided a little store and ate ice cream. The beer was too awful warm but the ice cream was at least served cold.

Two of the young squirts bought bottles of sassparilla extract thinking it was likker and I had to laugh so I told them what it was. On the way back through town two drunk sailors wanted to buy it so the boys sold it for $1 dollar and made a profit of 50 cents.

That is quite a pretty country but it was a little chilly and foggy although supposed to be summer they say but I can't figure that out as it is still February. Still some people were in swimming.

The next town we hit was Freemantle, Australia and it was quite warm there so we all went swimming. While we were swimming one day two sergeants snook away and come back with beer and wine in there shirts but the old man was wise and took it away from them but afterward gave it back. He is a pretty good guy at that. The people are nice but you can't understand them hardly as everybody always said goodie so I guess they never had any worries.

At this writing we are still at sea and the Captain says anyone who wanted to write a letter should do so now so it can be mailed at the next stop. I should tell you about our life on board here.

We are all in a stinking hole with canvas bunks four hight and eighteen inches acrossed. There is not much to do except read as we are allowed on deck only a few minutes per day. The last time it was my platoon's turn on deck, a swarm a Jap zeros came screaming out of nowhere, and we got plenty exercise diving into hatches to avoid the bullits, but didn't get any fresh air or sunshine at all. Just now we are all out of cigarettes and everybody is trying to mooch everybody else with no luck. It is a pretty sad deal. I am almost dying for a smoke.

Hoping you are the same, I remain,

Yours truly, **Gomer Fudd**

P.S. The last time anybody shot at me was in the other world war, and so I was reminded again about it:

#

General Quarters
November 30, 1917

We had been at sea for seven weeks except for brief stops at Brest and Brooklyn to pick up or deliver troops. We were definitely in the middle of the war and it was "hell." Mother Nature hadn't been very kind to us, either.

It seemed that the world had continued to fall apart. More nations had joined the fray; Brazil declared war and then a month later, revolution in Russia by the Bolsheviks.

With all the zigzagging and submarine alerts, it had been taking us more than twelve days to make a one-way crossing to France. We could dock, unload five thousand troops, reload some wounded and be headed back to the States in a record thirteen hours. When we were in convoy, we were usually the slowest vessel. All of the American and British destroyers and escorts could steam almost double our fourteen or fifteen knots.

Sometimes we were convinced that the weather was a greater enemy than the Germans. The North Atlantic gales of November were frightening, to say the least, and sometimes went on for days. The main deck of *Huron* was about thirty feet above the calm water line, but those fierce gales could produce waves that looked almost twice that height. When they washed over the decks it sounded like the ancient Greek god Thor was slamming the ship with his huge sledgehammer. The sound reverberated through the metal decks and bulkheads so that no part of the ship could escape the cacophony of sound. At times like that, no one was allowed on deck, except for emergencies, and then only if harnessed to a lifeline.

Our yeoman's office as I said earlier, was on the main deck, at the exact center of the ship, so the rolling, pitching and yawing caused by rough seas was somewhat lessened. Not exaggerated like in the outer extremities of the ship, i.e., the bow or the stern. Sometimes the listing could be so extreme that we thought this old tub was going to roll right over on her top. I had yet to figure out how she managed to right herself after these huge breakers almost rolled her over. One thing was certain, and that was that everything had to be secure, really battened down when it was like that. The only thing we couldn't secure was the contents of all the soldiers' stomachs, but at least the sea would eventually wash away all that stench.

One of our junior officers was a real sadistic sonofabitch. He took it upon himself to transfer three occupants of the brig to one of the forward rope lockers during one of the most severe storms we had yet encountered. Later, we all chuckled when he got a court-martial. It seems that the three prisoners got slammed around so bad up in the bow that they were all knocked out with concussions and had to be hospitalized.

After our second day of sea trials, we practiced convoy signals, zigzag routines and other evasive maneuvers. Admiral Jones had a hard time of it convincing some captains that the German U-boat threat was really out there. Left to their own devices, they probably would have sailed to France in a straight line, at a set speed and been picked off by Hun torpedoes like ducks in a shooting gallery.

When we did run the gauntlet, it would be with eight or ten merchantmen and a screen of destroyers. We traveled far to the north, under the "protection" of horrible weather, instead of taking a straight line to France, where the U-boats would expect us to be.

The drills we had to practice were to make sure all ships would "zig" at the same time. If only one quartermaster goofed up and "zagged" when he should have "zigged," there would be a collision for sure. None of those merchant marine captains were used to running so close to other ships anyway, which was the reason they were so hard to train to get it right. That's one reason that our captain hated having to drill with them. There were lots of other things those new wartime sailors would have to learn, before the war was over.

After two nights of drills, we returned to finish loading coal, then two days later, tied up of all places at the United States Steamship Lines dock on Staten Island. We no sooner got our hawsers flaked when gangways were lowered and troops started marching aboard. It amazed me to see how efficiently the troops boarded and disappeared below decks.

Normally, aboard ocean liners, the purser's office had the job of assigning people to quarters and arranging for all their needs. Aboard a warship, the yeoman's office doesn't have to do any of these duties, except keep personnel records for everyone on board.

The only records we kept then, was a list someone else had prepared of all the doughboys carried on each trip across the Atlantic. We loaded 5,321 army men and officers on that first trip, and got underway with them in less than fifteen hours.

Just past the lightship, we slowed and started to circle.

"What's wrong, now?" I asked Chief Turner.

"We have to wait for the escorts and for the convoy to get made up," he answered. "Our skipper doesn't believe there are any enemy submarines this close, but he's under orders."

Two hours later, it was just breaking daylight when *Huron* turned into the rising sun and increased speed. There was not another ship anywhere in sight.

"Skipper's grown impatient," offered the chief. "I sure hope he knows what he's doing…"

Then the bos'n's pipe blared, activating the all the speakers aboard. "Now hear this," he intoned, "Word from the bridge that orders have been received moving our rendezvous point out two hundred miles, because there aren't supposed to be any enemy submarines around."

That information should have caused a feeling of relief, but instead turned into instant fear. Many of the boys, experiencing their first time at sea, became at once apprehensive at this first mention of possible enemy submarines. There were some spontaneous dry mouths and some "gulping" sailors. Eyes kept drifting over the side and out to the horizon, distracted from assigned deck duties. And, sometimes the mind will play mean tricks on the eyes.

Well, as I said, we had a lot to learn. A fireman apprentice named Bill, who bunked in my section, convinced himself that he had seen a periscope and a conning tower. He hustled up to the bridge in a panic, seeking out the officer of the deck.

"Sir, I think I just saw a submarine!"

"You think you saw a sub? What's your name, sailor?"

"Bill."

Very annoyed, the officer bellowed, "What?"

"Fireman Apprentice William Worthy Creitz, SIR!"

I overheard this tense exchange and felt a pang of sorrow for my friend Bill. This was not the first time his overworked imagination would get him in trouble. Bill then disappeared somewhere into the bowels of the bridge structure, we assumed to get crapped on by the captain.

Imagine our surprise a few minutes later when they sounded general quarters! "This is not a drill," blared the loudspeakers. Bodies paused, and then jerked into instant chaos. It seemed for a split second that everyone was running amuck, until the instincts learned in many drills finally conquered the panic. We had drilled many times, but this was our first real test.

When I got to my battle station on the aft starboard gun, I had to settle my pounding heart, get it out of my throat and back where it belonged. Just as it settled down, someone spotted the wake of a torpedo coming from aft, right up our stern, and the panic started all over. The next couple of milliseconds froze in time and terror and none of us on the deck heard the cacophony of the collision siren sounding from the bridge.

It was instantly time to pray, and pray with meaning, because the wicked thing was aimed to strike right under our gun, and we had no time to do anything except to hold our breath... waiting, frozen in terror... In those few seconds, the pages of a man's life history flash before the mind's eye.

Tick! Click! The horrible tension peaked and everybody flinched!

A deafening silence followed... Red and purple lights flashed in my brain...

Time stood still. No closure! No climax!

Luck had been with us; the torpedo was a dud. It banked off our hull and harmlessly continued on into an open sea. The only casualties were some of the gun crew's drawers.

One of the destroyers making for our rendezvous point was close enough to answer our radio call, and we sighted her smoke about an hour later. We had to stay at general quarters for another six hours, but nothing further happened. We did hear some distant muffled depth-charge explosions later.

Towards sundown, when we were released from battle stations, the destroyer joined up with us and you better believe that our "old man" started to follow zigzag procedure. And Bill Creitz' validity and popularity was boosted by many notches.

An investigation into the incident determined that the sub had found us only because our mess cooks left a trail of floating garbage, which they dumped off the fantail after every meal. Dumping garbage and wastes at sea is something ships had always done, but now became a procedure that might require some re-thinking.

About midnight, we had teamed up with the rest of the convoy and made an uneventful crossing to a point off southern Ireland, where our escorts traded us off to some Brits.

We sailed southbound to the Bay of Biscay and the weather, wind and waves calmed somewhat. One morning, we could feel the ship slowing and went out on deck to see a glassy sea with real visible evidence of the war. We had been zigzagging through flotsam, evidence of blown-up ships.

One time the sea was covered with thousands of sacks of flour. We managed to pick up a few. The first inch or so outside was wet but the rest of the flour was in good condition.

We took two loads of doughboys to Brest during that month, but had no liberty at all. Our little ship's store ran out of everything on the first trip, and our boys were hurting for lots of stuff.

At sea, unless a man carried his own supply, he bought his smokes, candy and toiletries either from the ship's store or from the freelance merchants in the crew. Most of them charged shore-side prices, but I soon learned to not open my shop until all the others ran out, then charge up to a nickel each for a single cigarette.

Living and working topside in the yeoman's quarters gave me lots of extra advantages and I was lucky enough to have extra storage available, like the purser's walk-in vault which had been left intact when the ship had been converted. We also had almost three times the volume of personal lockers than the guys below decks.

Even before we were floated out of dry dock, I had realized the business potential, and had spent a whole month's pay to fill up two of my lockers with cigarettes, cigars, pipe tobacco, hard candy, some toiletries and a bunch of other stuff, including a lot of liquor. The liquor I locked up in the safe.

Sometimes in French harbors, "bumboats" came alongside and would sell the men almost anything, which always upset my business for a few days.

News from the front had been good. Our new command, formed earlier that month, was called the "Supreme Allied War Council." Their first joint effort supported a mostly British effort to break a hole almost five miles wide in the Hindenburg line at a place called Cambrai. They achieved it with a new armored truck called a "tank."

At the end of our next trip, we would be back home in New York for our first shore leave in almost two months, but not long enough for any real leave, just a short five or six hours of liberty, barely enough time to restock my hoard and maybe recapture the joy of Pearl's charms..   •

Chapter 6

Annies and Rubies
March 3, 1943

Dear Putzi:

Would you believe here I am in India where all the Indians come from but they aren't really red and are lots different than the Indians I use to know in the Yakima valley. I guess they're just like Germans and Swedes and Irishers and that kinda people and half to come to the United States to be civilized. This is some really weird county as everybody runs around with a turbine on his head and no pants hardly—only a sirloin.

We are at a British English camp but I cannot say where. We live in tents and half four meals a day which are not enough to keep a mosquito alive. We sleep under mosquito bars and that reminds me of a story one of the boys told. There was these two mosquitos setting on the end of his bunk talking, and one said shall we eat him here or carry him out into the jungle. The other one said oh we better eat him here because one of them big fellas will take him away from us out there in the woods. I don't really think this is true.

This is strictly a rest camp as we half natives to do almost everything. They will even shave you in bed for about two cents and some of them carry little pots of tea and cake around and holler tea-walla, tea-walla, lovely tea. We have a boot-walla to shine our shoes and a sweep-walla to do our work around the tent and when we aren't sleeping we drink tea and sometimes have strumpets with it while we wait for the shave-walla. We call our boot-walla Gunga-dung because somebody named Ripley wrote a poem about him one of the boys said.

I better explain about wallas before I go any farther. Everybody that works which isn't many is a walla of some kind. A gharry-walla drives a gharry; a tea-peddler is a tea-walla or a chow-walla; a fella that sells cattle is a buffalo-walla and an employment agency fella must be a Walla-Walla I guess.

I cannot tell you the name of the port where we come to land at because that is also unmentionable on account of the senser but we had a good time anyhow. We went for a ride in a gharry which is kind of a one-horse four-in-hand. We went all over town and the gharry-walla took us to all the places of historic interest, especially the street of the wailing virgins where some historic speciments are kept in cages. Some people say that the virgins are virgins just from the neck up but that don't make no sense to me. They all held up there fingers in the V sign so they must be very patriotic but we had an argument because one fella said it meant two Rubies to do business and another fella said it meant the scope of there repetory or something like that. Anyhow speaking of two Rubies that is what a Tom Collins costs. I will now explain about Rubies as one Ruby is worth sixteen Annus and one Annie is good for 4 piece, so a piece is pretty cheap in India because a Ruby is worth about 30 cents American. I don't know if I spelt them right.

In the same town was innumerous beggars all crying for buckshee as they call it. Some of them were pitiful sights but we were told to void them and anyhow I couldn't possibly have enough Annus to go around.

I bought a knife for ten Rubies which one of the boys said was a very good knife providing I didn't try to cut anything harder than butter. I saw lots of strange sights expecially a snake dancing while an Indian played some kind of ocarina. The snake was a *cobra de capello* but one of the boys said that de capello was Italian and meant without an organ. Well, I suppose a flute does just as well or an ocarino.

One of the boys borrowed me a little book which he got in a cartoon of Woodbine cigarettes so I am able to explain all about India and Indians which is altogether different than the United States. They have four seasons which are winter, summer, monsoon and curry. Now is late summer and we will get a monsoon sun soon which means no sun at all. Winter was before summer and curry is any old time they say but that don't make no sense to me either.

They have lots of mountains and rivers here. The biggest rivers are the Gangrene and the Brahmaputrid and the mountains are up at Shanker-la.

There are over twenty-three thousand different sex in India and they must think a lot of it as they even call there money after girls names and things as I explained before. A woman of one sex cannot marry one of another and vive voce. They also have a lot of casks which I do not understand very much about but they all have a mark on there forehead and it ain't triple xxx. They even have a separate cask for emptying the sewerage, etc. Some are very proud of there cask mark but most are not and let it be covered with dirt so the neighbors can't see it.

I can't tell you much about the habits of the Indians except they chew something called beetle nuts and spit red. Also it is hard to tell a man from a woman from the rear as they all dress sorta the same and both squat when they relieve themselves.

We have been cautioned not to get deceased: "Don't drink water so you won't get disentory.

"Don't let mosquitos bite you so you won't get malaria.

"Don't handle parrots so you won't get parrotonitus, etc." We have been inculcated for everything from belly-ake to lackanooki which is also a topical decease but some of the boys said that the last one didn't take so they are now suffering from that decease. Hoping you are the same, I remain,

Yours truly, *Gomer Fudd*

P.S. Speaking of "lackinooki", this life here is worse than when I was sailing back and forth across the Atlantic in the last war. At least I got to see Pearl once in a while. Reminisce with me back to yesteryear:

#

Sweet Revenge, Maybe?
December 26, 1917

We were at sea again, having left New York City at 3:00 a.m. on December 26th. There were an awful lot of upset people, sad at missing Christmas, but troops were so badly needed in France and elsewhere that everyone understood the sacrifice. All messes did manage a pretty good turkey dinner, which helped.

That was our fifth trip across the Atlantic and we loaded over six thousand marines and a company of nurses. Up until then, we had hauled only army soldiers, but on this trip there were only a couple of dozen army stragglers. They were mostly unassigned, traveling alone, under individual orders, attempting to catch up with units that had already been hauled across. So, not having any commanding officers, we had to process their orders for delivery to certain commands in Brest, St. Nazaire and elsewhere.

The morning after departure, I got my first look at some of the orders, and who should be aboard but my old enemy Luke Lufkin! He's the army thief who stole my wallet and then conned Poops into arresting me for it. Reading his orders, I learned that he had been hospitalized from a barroom brawl and missed his billet on a ship the month before. He was aboard at the time, hoping to catch up with his buddies before they got to the front.. I had about ten days to dream up my revenge and send him somewhere nasty. Heh, heh! And, I did it too, scoundrel that I was.

The first thing I did was to get him transferred to "temporary scullery duties," where he had to move in with the cooks and stewards, who were mostly Negro.[3] Lufkin hated that because he was from the Deep South and probably had some racial prejudices of his own. As he was under no onboard officer's command, it was easy for me to forge a signature on his orders. And, his punishment had only begun! My joy was that he didn't have the foggiest idea that I was aboard, let alone what was happening to him.

I'm not all bad. I'd been studying for the yeoman first class test, and still had some of the notes that I secretly copied from yeoman's mate school, which would be a big help. I'd be eligible to take the exam in a month (As long as some wise guy didn't discover that I'm not as old as my service record says). Mutt and Jeff were also studying and I helped them along for their third class exam; the one I never had to take. Once they got promoted to petty officer third class, they would be able to move into the yeoman's quarters and not be detailed to deck duties all the time by the boatswain.

Earlier that month, the United States declared war on Austria-Hungary and the British finally captured Jerusalem, which showed how really widespread that stinking war was. We had been pretty lucky, though. The last trip across, we only had to go to battle stations twice, for real. All the other times were drills. We saw no action at all, since that first trip's torpedo scare. And you better believe that the mess cooks were now weighing down the garbage in bags with heavy ballast before pitching it overboard.

After that last trip, I did manage to get a few hours sampling the joys of Pearl. She was a nice lady, but I thought she was a little disappointed in me because I wouldn't talk marriage. I was still too young to be tied down to only one woman and she really burst my bubble at the dock when we said goodbye.

Just as I started up the gangway, she reached over, as if to nibble on my ear, but instead she whispered, "No more poon-tang for you, sailor boy, unless you want it permanent."

Damn!

There was nothing to be had "free" in France, either. The French girls got you three ways; they took your money, they stole your heart and then left your joystick dripping with disease. We were constantly warned, but most of the men still came back with syphilis or some other crutch.

We made our first liberty in Brest, France. From the anchorage, the town looked picture post-card alluring: with an old chateau overlooking the harbor, the steep roofs of buildings, and the church steeples breaking the horizon of rooftops. We were not allowed much time, and were most impatient as our motor-sailer queued up waiting to follow the other boats into the narrow harbor to the landing. In the dark, we climbed the long flight of steps to the Rue de Siam, and looked back over the moonlit harbor. There were ships of all kinds and nationalities: transports, freighters, cruisers, destroyers, all types of auxiliaries, and another type of craft new to me—the wooden submarine chasers. With all this buildup of men and materials, the end of the war should have been in sight, or so we reflected.

We barely had time to get a decent drunk started before we were called back to the ship.

In addition to American, I now carried tobacco products from France, England and Russia.

I thought I might write down some more navy terminology from what I'd been able to learn:

"Smoking Lamp": During the sixteenth century, the smoking lamp was a safety measure designed to provide a candle flame for lighting smoking tobacco at the only designated smoking place aboard sailing vessels. Because of highly combustible woodwork, hemp, and gunpowder, smoking was only permitted on the forecastle, near the galley, so a covered lamp was kept there. If the lamp was not lit, sailors could not smoke. The smoking lamp has survived only as a figure of speech. When the officer of the deck says, "The smoking lamp is out" before drills, refueling or taking on ammunition, that is the Navy's way of saying, "Cease smoking."

We couldn't smoke for the four days it took to fill up the coal bunkers, because the coal dust was so fine, any spark would have caused an explosion. Not much other work could be done during that time either, as that fine black dust seeped into everything, so all vents and doors (hatches) were shut and kept closed except for emergencies.

"Port" and *"Starboard"*: Left and right respectively or "zig" and "zag" respectively. Any confusion could cause a shipwreck. In old England, the starboard was the steering paddle or rudder, and ships were always steered from the right side on the aft of a vessel. *"Larboard"* referred to the left side, the side on which the ship was loaded. Larboard became "port" because shouting over the noise of wind and waves, larboard and starboard sounded too much alike and caused confusion. The U. S. Navy officially adopted the term "port" in 1846.

All the downtime due to the coaling operation had given me plenty of think time to figure out where I was going to get Lufkin shipped off to.

#

After Pearl demanded "permanent payment" for services performed, I dropped her like a hot potato, so I guess I should tell you about the new girl I'd met. She was a real knockout named Winnie, and is a close cousin of Cecil Martin.

Ah, yes, you should remember my best friend Cecil from recruit camp? He was a quartermaster's mate. Well, in January, when *Huron* was tied up at the Brooklyn Navy Yard, taking on another load of soldiers, I was sitting at my desk, processing a huge pile of orders, when a loud, angry knocking came from the hatch (doorway). I didn't bother to look around to see who it was, but simply called out, "Enter."

"So you're the pimp whot screwed up me orders!" shouted a strained voice.

Fearing instant reprisals from one of my earlier "victims," I turned around, defensively prepared for rebuttal.

"I've gotcha now, Pete," continued the voice from a unrecognizable face, shadowed because the bright sun was directly at his back.

"B-But…" stammered I, just beginning to realize that the body in the doorway was too big to be anyone I had screwed up before, and was instead…

"Cecil! You old sea stud," I exclaimed. "Is it really you?"

"Yup, and I've just been transferred to this old tub."

We had a great time catching up with each other's careers. Cecil had been sent to a destroyer flotilla right out of the training center, and had just had his ship blown right out from under him by a German torpedo, and had requested re-assignment to something not so hazardous.

On our next short leave, he said to me, "Come on, Pete, my Aunt Gladys in the Bronx will welcome us—and she has several lovely daughters." That was enough incentive for me, who by then was really missing female companionship.

It was away out in the country, almost a farm, and it cost us a bundle in fares to get there. The trip was most time-consuming; first a ferry from Brooklyn to Manhattan, then the elevated train to the Bronx, then a horse car for three miles, then we had to walk another two miles.

Cecil's aunt was a gracious lady and we had a grand time. She introduced me to her three daughters, Winnie, Imogene and Rachel. After an excellent meal, the best I'd had in over a year, we gathered around the piano and sang all the old songs until late in the evening. The middle girl, Imogene, was very shy but had a spectacular voice and she also played the piano for us.

When it was time to leave, I winked at Winnie and promised to take her to the upcoming Valentine's Day dance. We thought we were scheduled to be in port then.

Our turn-around times had slowed down considerably. While we still crossed the ocean in eleven or twelve days, the pressure was off about fast turn-around times, and we now usually had two or three days in port preparing for the next trip. Last month, a lot of soldiers arrived two days early, so they got put to work shoveling coal.

Now my devious mind had time to ponder more mischief and you all are just dying to know what I did with Luke Lufkin.

There was a chance that I could have cut my own throat by writing all this down, but it was worth it.

First, I burned his army orders and dumped the ashes overboard, then wrote up replacements putting him on long-term "loan" to the British Navy at Scapa Flow, Scotland. He would think that the high command was punishing him for fighting and missing his billet. There was a great shortage of support people to do an extremely important and urgent job in Scapa Flow. Because it was so cold there, it was one of the few places where that particular job could be done properly, and Luke Lufkin should have been proud to lend a hand to help out all the British heroes. So, I felt that I was really doing him a favor: He'd be spending the duration of the war preparing corpses for burial.

My revenge would have been a lot sweeter if there had been any way I could have let him know the truth, but I couldn't take that chance. At least the poor slob wouldn't get sunburned up there in the frozen North.

57

In February, I kept my word and made it to the dance with Winnie. We had a seventy-two-hour pass, and after three straight days with her I was not sure if I wanted to keep seeing her or not. She bossed me around like my mother and could be overbearing sometimes. Maybe it's because she was older than I was. I liked her a lot because she was so gregarious. But sometimes also she could be too brazen.

As I said earlier, that little Imogene was a real cutie, smart as a whip and really shy. I liked that. Also, she was more my own age and respected me. She was someone that I could introduce to my parents with pride. Also, I'd learned not to be so selfish about taking my own pleasure, but to slow down, as those girls scare off easily.

I passed my first-class yeoman's exam, but Chief Turner said that I couldn't have the promotion without making a transfer to another ship where there is a vacancy.

"If you want the promotion, I'll be happy to send you to some warship," he said, "but you know that I'd rather keep you here." He had proven to be kind of a lazy man, anyway, and didn't want to lose me, because I did most of his work in addition to my own.

"Besides," he added, "you're making more money scamming the crew and the troops than you could ever make aboard a warship." He was referring, of course, to my lockers full of cigarettes and candy. I wasn't sure if he knew about the contraband booze, but if he suspected anything he kept it to himself. You know, scratch my back and I'll scratch yours. It was an attribute that all on board had to learn to practice for their survival.

Since the first of that year, we had made six round trips to France, two to Saint Nazaire, and four to Brest. The war map reminded me of two throbbing amoebae that one might view in a laboratory microscope. They grew, then shrunk, pulsed and shimmered with reproductive activity. In March, Germany had been advancing everywhere, defeating Russia and moving to within thirty-two miles of Paris, but then, the lines changed and changed again.

Then, a Frenchman, General Ferdinand Foch, was appointed the Supreme Allied Commander. The British bombarded two German U-Boat bases, and the submarines that constantly threatened us were supposed to have been beaten.

A few weeks before, the German armies had been pushed back by French and British troops. The big guns in France, it was said, could no longer be heard in the English Channel. By the next spring, everyone thought the front should collapse. And, best of all, the submarines were supposed to have been licked. But we were mistaken.

On our last trip to Brest, we were held over for an extra couple of days, so most of the boys got a few hours' liberty. Chief Turner and I had to make an unexpected courier trip to the French commander at Nantes, with a pouch full of secret documents. Nantes was upriver a couple hours' drive from Brest. We were given a fast truck, a French driver and two armed marines. After we delivered our packet of information, we took a little time to eat and enjoy a glass of red wine, before returning to the ship.

Two days later, as we were getting up steam, French newspaper headlines were screaming, *"La grippe en Nantes!"*

The chief and I were ordered to the bridge.

"Did you eat or drink anything in Nantes?" barked the skipper.

"Yes, sir!"

"Too bad," he said, "I'm going to have to quarantine you in your quarters effective immediately until the ship's doctor can clear you." Distracted briefly to give orders to his helmsman, he turned back to us and continued, "It's a major influenza outbreak and you two were right in the middle of it. Now, get out of here!"

That was on 23 April, 1918. Chief Turner and I returned to quarters and ordered Mutt and Jeff out. The carpenter had arrived and cut a little pass through in our hatchway, so we could receive food and water. Then, he padlocked the door shut with a new hasp on the outside. We were literally prisoners.

"Guess we'll get caught up on reading and writing," I suggested.

"Call up and see if you can get an acey-deucy board sent down," Turner asked. Acey-deucy was Navy slang for backgammon.

The next day, the chief complained of a fever and we had to call the boatswain to unlock our door so the medical staff could check him out.

Within a few minutes, Doc Walker himself was let in, stating he couldn't trust the job to any corpsman. After a few "hm-ms" and "tsks," he told the chief to gather up whatever he wanted because his quarantine had to be continued in the sick bay isolation ward.

After he was gone, I realized that I was locked in there all alone, and the business of keeping all ship's records was still mine to do alone. A daunting task!

Every hour, I felt my forehead, looking for any sign of temperature…
anything to get out of all that work! But, I continued to feel fine, the whole ten
days it took to return to New York City. On the day before we dropped anchor,
I heard the screws in the hasp being removed and Doc Walker came by to visit.

"You're in the clear, Pete," he informed me, "and the quarantine has been
lifted." Then he glanced in the direction of my supply lockers and with a wink,
said, "I bet you'll have a drink to that!"

I poured us both a stout one and we savored every drop.

"What about Chief Turner?" I asked with real concern.

He turned away, and cleared his throat.

"I'm afraid Turner's in trouble," he began. "He contracted pneumonia, and
I'm shipping him to the naval hospital at Newark when we dock tomorrow."

He paused, then coughed before continuing, "I don't think he's going to
make it, Pete. In any event, as senior rating, you'll have to carry the load here,
until his replacement arrives."

My head was spinning out of control, faster than this crazy world, and not
from the booze, either. How could a lying, cheating, kid with barely one year's
naval service be thrust into the responsibility of accountant in charge of the
service records and lives of 440 sailors? Our boss, Lieutenant (jg) McHenry
didn't know the first thing about bookkeeping, accounting, filing BuNav
reports, promotional requirements, supply inventories or transfer orders. I
didn't even think he could use a typewriter.

I called down for Mutt and Jeff to get up there and help bail me out of ten
days' accumulated paperwork. A later conference with Lieutenant McHenry
and the skipper allowed me to approve Mutt and Jeff's promotion to third-class
petty officers, effective that same day. They were pleased, and moved their
stuff into our yeoman's quarters. The first thing we did was to pack up Chief
Turner's stuff. It was done neatly and with respect and ceremony as we all
loved the old chief and were sorry to be losing him. The old purser's quarters
had been equipped with four pull-down bunks, so we still had one to spare.

The next day we docked, but not long enough for all of us to go ashore. Both
of them were required to man the office while we were dockside. It's sure was
great to be the boss, yeah!

#

Just when the real transformation happened is something I often thought about, but knew that I'd never find an answer. Just how and when did this innocent Iowa farm boy turn inwardly selfish? I used to serve as an altar boy and knew my catechism forward and backwards. I'd a much greater education than most other kids from the Midwest. When my Scottish Presbyterian Pa found work, we kids were all forced into Saint Aloysius Catholic School. I guess something important was missing, because my faith had always been shallow.

In the World War One Navy I was really "grown up" and could "con" almost anyone into believing anything. Take those beautiful young ladies that I was so nuts about. If they knew the real me inside, they'd flee in terror, or was I just "conning" myself with unnecessary melancholy?

Right then in that story, Imogene had stolen my heart and I was overwhelmed with emotion about her. We had been at sea again, about a third of the way over to France, with another load of doughboys, and in my reverie I just had to write some of this down.

Those lonely hours at sea passed quickly when I reveled in the thoughts of all the fun Imogene and I had in the last few days I was in port. A picnic and hayride was one that I would never forget, and I wrote a letter to my "Shimmy Immy" and a little ditty about it which went like this:

Often I think of that time in May
And all that it means to me;
Often my thoughts in fancy stray
To my barren life before that day,
And the future's mystery
***

I can see the bright sun's fitful glow
Through the canopy of trees;
I remember the river down below
That shimmered in iridescent flow,
And the scent of the fragrant breeze.
***

I remember the sky of azure hue,
And the birds and the butterflies;
And all the beauty of Heaven's blue

Whose lambent tints were transferred to
The magic of your eyes!
***

And as we returned, and the setting sun
Shone with a fire sublime,
Although you thought it was all in fun,
My heart told me that we were one,
One till the end of time!

My letter probably wouldn't reach her until we returned to New York, and by that time, I'd HOPED I'd be able to see her again in person, but everybody knows how the fickle fortunes of war can interfere with the progress of a new relationship.

I was so very glad that her cousin Cecil, who was also my best friend, had been able to go along and be a companion to her sister. I hoped that Winnie was not too sore at me for wanting to date Imogene instead. Then there was the Friday night dance that was a real whammy! I wondered where in the world did Imogene learn to shimmy the way that she did? Memories of her close, warm vibrating body would be with me forever, and I couldn't wait until the ship came back to Brooklyn so I could see her again. Oh, joy! I heard her mom shorten her name to "Immy"; so, from then on she was my "Shimmy Immy."

There was a sonnet that I penned for just such a time as that:

Dear! Of all happy in the hour, most blest
He who has found our hid security,
Assured in the dark tides of the world at rest,
And heard our word, "Who is so safe as we?"
We have found safety with all things undying,
The winds, and morning, tears of men and mirth,
The deep night, and birds singing, and clouds flying,
And sleep, and freedom, and the autumnal earth.
***
We have built a house that is not for Time's throwing.
We have gained a peace unshaken by pain forever.
War knows no power. Safe shall be my going,

> *Secretly armed against all death's endeavor;*
> *Safe though all safety's lost; safe where men fall;*
> *And if these poor limbs die, safest of all.*[4]

Before we left port, I expected Chief Turner's replacement to come aboard, but that didn't happen. Instead, the skipper informed me that BuNav had approved my promotion to first-class yeoman, which meant a raise in pay of almost four dollars a month and another stripe on my uniform. I still had to do all my regular duties plus that of the chief yeoman's mate. But I had two "cracker-jack" helpers, though, so guessed that I'd get by.

Chapter 7

Hotman Gandy
March 5, 1943

Dear Putzi:

This is a tough life in this here camp. All I half to do is be on time for meals so here goes another letter in two days. I will tell you all about the history of India which I remember from that little cigarette paper book.

According to the Indus a fella named Budday started it all because he lived a normal life with his wife and family until he was thirty and then he left home to search for ha'penis and set under a tree looking at his belly button and didn't wash. All the Indians thought that was a good idea so they made him a saint.

But pretty soon a lot of fellas had other ideas most of which meant to keep the lower casks in there places so Budday moved out and a fella named Shivar took over. He believed that a man should take a bath once in the summer and not quite so often in winter.

He also believed it was unlawful to take any life, even a louse or an ant or a flea or even a mosquito. He also tried to raise Indus with six different arms so they could yell for buckshee from six different suckers at one time.

But now the whole business has been turned over to a fella named Hotman Gandy that teaches the people about passive resistance and stuff that means that everybody should lay on the sidewalk and not work. The Indians really like that idea so Gandy is a very popular fella.

In the meantime the British English took over about 200 years ago on account of they half to have tea and this was a good place to grow it. At first they had a little trouble for instance one time a rajah put the whole bunch of them in a dark cellar with only one small widow the book says and the next morning only four of them was alive. It must have been a black widow because they still call it the Black Hole of Calcutta.

Another time they had a siege at a place called Lucknow and just when the people were almost starving a girl called out the Camels are coming so the Indian soldiers grounded there butts and had a real smoke. Speaking of Camels, the British English have four thousand different brands of cigarettes which all taste like timothy hay that has passed through a horse and I wish we had some real Camels or even some Luckies to smoke.

About ninety years ago they had quite rebellion known as the Sepoy rebellion. The Sepoys were native Indian soldiers who were working for the British English and one time they introduced a new food ration called corned beef which had such a hard crust around it that most of the Sepoys broke there teeth trying to bite it. Finally they put some in a cannon and shot it off which happened to kill some British Englishmen and started the revolution. The British English soon won out and they tied every tenth Sepoy to the mouth of a cannon and shot him off in what is called the process of decimation and is where we get our decimal system. At least that is what my first sergeant says and he went to high school.

My first sergeant is a pretty nice fella. He says that one of these days we will get together and write about all the bugs and things as this country is sure buggy. I hope you remain the same,

Yours truly, *Gomer Fudd*

P.S. It was about this time that I got promoted to Corporal, which reminded me about a big and unearned promotion that I got in the First World War:

\#

Chief
August 3, 1918

What a terrific and wonderful summer Shimmy Immy and I had doing things together. It was not over yet, but I was afraid that I would have to miss seeing her for a month or so.

On August 2nd, just before leaving Saint Nazaire, a chief yeoman named Roger Daythan came aboard, and surprised me. Replacement men always came aboard in home port, never from overseas.

"I'm only temporary," Chief Daythan said, "because I'm just hitching a ride back to the States so I can retire and go run a hog and chicken ranch."

He handed me several packets of orders, including one with my name on it.

"What's this?" I queried.

"I'm only replacing you for one and a half trips," he said. "They want you to teach me the special syncs of this ship, so I can take her over and back one time while you are in chief petty officer school."

"Wow!" I stammered. "That means…?"

"Yup," he interrupted, "you're going to be a chief yeoman and were picked by BuNav to be Turner's replacement. Congratulations!" He held out his hand in friendship.

But I hugged him instead, which turned his face a little pink.

"Sorry, Chief," I blushed, "I just got carried away."

"That's okay," he replied.

Then he mumbled something I didn't quite catch, like, "I've spent my whole navy career wet-nursing 'em and now I'm going to learn how to raise 'em… pigs, that is!"

I was so filled with pride. Pride to share with my darling Immy; the next time she'd see me, I would be wearing the uniform of a chief petty officer!

Was this to be a foretaste of power and success? Would my devious ways continue to produce prestige and fortune?

I was so glad that both of our families avoided catching that terrible "Springtime" grippe. They knew for sure that it was a new strain of influenza, and had shortened the name down to "flu" (or "flue"; I'm not sure which). Whatever they called the pandemic, it had killed millions of people all over the world. The latest count of deaths in the United States was well over 175,000 and still rising.

I read in the newspapers about that one battle in the trenches between an American division and a German battalion. More than half on each side had that flu, and after close hand-to-hand combat, everybody who didn't die in combat caught the flu and died anyway. What a waste this war was! The line still held, and neither side gained an inch of ground.

When was it? Around the first of June, I think, when the first all-American operation captured Cantigny. I guess we proved that we worked better alone. Anyway, just after that, all the remaining neutral nations started declaring war on Germany in rapid succession. There was Guatemala, Nicaragua, Costa Rica, Haiti, Honduras and a whole bunch of others. If I could really pray, I would have prayed that the war must end soon.

I couldn't wait to get back into Emmy's loving embraces and feel her soft smooth skin again. Oh, joy!

Emmy wrote letters now almost every day. One day at mail call, I was a little embarrassed when they called out a letter for "Popeye Pete." It was so heavily perfumed that the whole ship could smell it. Boy, did my face turn red! Letters, of course, get all bunched up and we only got mail when in home port. While at sea, however, I wrote to her and included verse, like:

If, sweetheart, you cannot sleep And you tire of counting sheep,
Try the countless stars to number, This should surely bring on slumber.
If you still are wide awake, Count the drops that fill a lake,
If this fails and sleep has missed you,
Count the times that I have kissed you!
If sweet slumber still does thwart, Try this for a last resort:
It will make your senses numb, Count the kisses still to come!

* * *

August 11, 1918: It was still too early in the season for one of those famous North Atlantic raging gales that they liked to tell the wild tales about. So why did we get orders to batten everything down for what they said was to be "the storm of the century"?

Officers always enjoyed scaring the pee out of raw young sailors, and we had lots of new recruits aboard. Maybe it would be just another initiation. We were about halfway between Newfoundland and home when I began to believe there might be something to the warnings, as the sea was really beginning to rise and the wind blowing something fierce.

After another hour, that old tub *Huron* had started to buck like a bronco and was rolling from side to side in some pretty deep troughs. It occurred to me that if I knew anything about seamanship, the skipper had better turn us into the waves pretty soon, or we were going to capsize. I thought it odd that there was no rain, only wind and high sea. I dug out my trusty old Kodak, and while waiting for the next huge wave, began to realize how terrified I was. The yeoman's office is located on an upper deck, only one level below the bridge, so the view out our port was pretty spectacular. Even Chief Daythan, a seasoned sailor, was nervous. Beyond the next trough, I could see the next monster wave, headed broadside to our portside. My hand holding the camera was shaking as we started to slide down into the trough. The wave on the other side was gigantic, easily more than one hundred feet high, and when it slammed into the side of the ship, I thought it was curtains. The sound alone was a cacophony of shrieking metal under stress, and the concussion knocked me down into unconscious oblivion.

With a roaring headache, I next awoke in the ship's infirmary, glad to be alive. One of my first sensations told me we were on calm seas, so the storm must have passed.

"How long have I been here?" I weakly managed to ask

"Only twelve hours," a corpsman told me. "You're lucky, down in the starboard mess, three sailors died." After full recovery, we learned that our freak storm was the remains of a tropical hurricane that had killed over six hundred people. I would have liked to show off pictures of that monster wave, but I later found where the shock of it had sent my trusty old Kodak flying across the room and smashed into a million pieces against the opposite bulkhead.

As soon as we docked from that trip, I caught a train up to Portsmouth for a three-week school. I thought that if I could hurry through school and beat *Huron* back to Brooklyn, I might get a chance to see my Immy before we had to shove off again.

September 11, 1918: Who would ever believe it? I had been in this man's Navy for only a year and a half, and was already a chief petty officer. That was as high as an enlisted man could go without extra schooling and longevity. That warrant officer promotion was one I'd never consider, because when this war was over and my "tour" was up, I'd be for a discharge. There were too many sheep landside, just waiting to be fleeced. I'd proven that my abilities to advance myself were extraordinary, so I'd already set some new goals. Foremost was that I'd be a millionaire by the time I reached twenty-five!

The CPO conferences up in Portsmouth lasted a week longer than I had planned on, and by the time my train got back to Brooklyn, *Huron* was already at her dock and I was ordered to report aboard immediately. And that's why I didn't get to see my Shimmy Immy that month at all. If there were any way I could have sneaked off that tub to spend a few hours with her, I'd have done it. I just had to settle for a nice long letter instead and get it mailed before we sailed. By the time she received it, we'll already be on the way back to France.

The officer of the deck knew me too well, believing that I would sneak off if I could, and had put an extra watch on the yeoman's office. I would have even risked losing my brand-new rating to see her.

Chief Daythan left the office and my work in a mess, doing only what work he had to. He'd already gone, headed for the discharge separation unit, anxious to end his thirty-five-year career.

Mutt and Jeff had done what they could, but I was going to have to completely restructure the duty roster in the office. I found it difficult to concentrate on my duties, so wrote a song to Immy, instead:

(Verse 1):
This is what I vow: She shall have my heart to keep;
Sweetly will we stir and sleep,
All the years, as now. Swift the measured sands may run; Love like
this is never done;
She and I are welded one; This is what I vow.
(Verse 2):
This is what I pray: Keep her by me tenderly;
Keep her sweet in pride of me, Ever and a day;
Keep me from the old distress; Let me, for our happiness,
Be the one to love the less
This is what I pray.
(Verse 3):
This is what I know: Lover's oaths are thin as rain;
Love's a harbinger of pain ...
Would it were not so!
Ever is my heart a-thirst, Ever is my love accursed;
She is neither last nor first ...
This is what I know.

#

The Armistice was signed on November 13, 1918, but there at sea, we didn't get the word until two nights later. Our captain wanted to stop the ship mid-ocean and have a party, but the convoy commodore refused.

"Absolutely not!" he signaled back. "Hun subs are still out there and may not know the war is over…"

We could have predicted that the war would end within five or six weeks of September 27th. That's the day the Allies finally broke through the Hindenberg Line.

But we still had a party, everybody except the lookouts and the duty watch. Because we were on the return leg, we had only a couple of hundred soldiers aboard, so the stewards set up in the main dining salon. They broke out some hoarded champagne, and when that was gone, we got one tot of rum per man, courtesy of our beloved captain.

The returning doughboys were the life of the party… we even had five nurses, who must have danced with fifty men each. I'd bet that they were exhausted.

In addition to the popular "Mademoiselle from Armenteers," soldiers taught us a few other songs they had learned from the British. One to the tune of: "Take it to the Lord in Prayer" went like this:

When this bloody war is over, O, how happy I shall be!
When I get my civvy clothes on, No more soldiering for me.
No more church parades on Sunday, No more asking for a pass,
I shall tell the sergeant major to stick his passes up his arse.
I shall sound my own reveille, I shall make my own tattoo:
No more NCO's to curse me, No more bleeding army stew. [5]

After we left the main party, we had a continuation up in the yeoman's office, courtesy of yours truly, who still had a locker full of booze. Mutt and Jeff, of course, because they lived there, and Cecil Martin, who was lucky enough not to have duty, and then there were two seaman strikers that had been assigned to me. One of them brought along one of the nurses. And I couldn't understand why she wouldn't dance with anyone… And I couldn't remember who else, but there were at least four other guys. Anyway, we had a full house for a while, until the officer of the deck, a smarty-pants ensign, put everybody on report for, he said, "disturbing the peace."

The next week, we were due to dock and I sure hoped we would get to refit and take some R and R. That old tub was getting tired, and so were most of the crew. She was going to need the barnacles scraped off her bottom and some new paint. So, if Lady Luck survived, I'd get to see my sweet "Shimmy Immy" and maybe even do some shimmying!

It was hard to realize that would be the completion of our eighth round-trip to France and back.

I didn't share with Immy yet how Lady Fortune had indeed been so kind to me. Specifically about my rapid promotions, my earnings from contraband whiskey and cigarettes, and the little payroll scheme I did for Lieutenant Househoder that had left me with some "extra cash" which I had to then consider investing in the future. I was to be out of this man's Navy in a little less than a year and if I were going to reach my newest goal, I'd be in need a good productive job. I'd given a lot of thought to various scams and needed to be on the lookout for something productive, dealing with investing money, accounting, bookkeeping, payroll or banking.

W. C. Fields once said that there's a sucker born every minute and I believed there were lots of suckers out there, just waiting to be fleeced. There was a stoker down in the black gang, named Bill Creitz, from Portland, Oregon, who had some ideas he wanted to share. He had been looking for a partner. Something to do with selling partnership investments, and I thought I'd better listen to what he had to say.

Shimmy Immy was such an object of my affection that she made me wax poetic. I was working on a verse to celebrate the end of the war, but was stumped with it ... because when I closed my eyes to compose a line, all I could see was her!

> *I think, sweetheart, 'most every night, when I am low and blue.*
> *That I'm not good enough to write about the charms of you.*
> *The poets great, with golden pens, should take the task in hand,*
> *And get your likeness in a lens so I could understand.*
> *I rave about your lovely hair, and of your sparkly eyes...*
> *I have no literary flair, and never passing wise.*
> *'Twould be an easy thing for one who's reached poetic fame,*
> *To write of you, and when he's done immortalize your name.*
> *The famous poets all could glut their eyes on you, and write*
> *A masterpiece of beauty, but you must admit, they're right!*

#

71

I often found myself "praying" to some unknown:

"Please, dear Fates, don't ever allow a conflict between my bad side 'Joekel' goals and my good side 'Hyde's' love life. I could never bear to have Immy find out about my shady side. She would be so hurt."

Chapter 8

Brahmaputrid
April 14, 1943

Dear Putzi:

Well, here we are in another British English camp as we have been riding on a troop train for days and days and sleeping on slats. The country was not very interesting all flat and cut into little tiny farms.

We saw some banana trees and monkies and lots of beggars. This camp is very small and all we half to do is wait for a river boat. I think this is the Brahmaputrid river so as I have nothing else to do I will drop you a short note.

These British English camps are sure crumby as the chow is terrible and all we have to wash our mess kits in is a pail of cold greasy water and the latrines are a crying shame which make your eyes smart. I hope we wind up in a good old American camp.

In this place they have some dive bombing hawks which can snatch a hunk of bacon out of your mess kit before you know what it is all about and can drop a bomb on your helmet with pin-point accuracy. They are very smart and usually pick on the officers although sometimes they will condescend to attack a non com.

My first sergeant said, "Non com is abbreviation for *non compis mentis* which is a Latin military phrase." But he couldn't remember what it meant because he had forgot his Caesar.

Well, the boys are organizing a soft ball game so I must quit. I am sorry that this letter is so short and uninteresting. Hoping you are the same, I remain
Yours truly, *Gomer Fudd*

P. S. Laying in my bunk at night when it's too hot to sleep, and I'm bored out of my gourd, I like to recall some of the good old times and fun that I had in the last war:

#

The Theresa Bear Caper
February 14, 1919

Valentine's Day is a day for lovers all over the world. I was so disgusted that day in 1919, because I was missing my Shimmy Immy so very much. We all thought that when the war ended, everything would slow down, and we could have more time for shore leave. Not so, and I'm sure she was feeling the disgust of separation also.

The danged marines and doughboys were getting their "rewards" then, but we had to work all that much harder, just to get them all home again. Our turn-around times were now just about as bad as they were when we first started.

There was still some U-boat activity for a couple of weeks after the armistice was signed, even for a couple of days after the German High Fleet surrender on November 21st. No Allied ship was allowed to stop the zigzag evasions until well into January. Then we could make better time crossing.

I had to laugh to myself, when I heard that the whole Hun navy surrendered to the British at Scapa Flow, and I wonder how much extra work detail might have involved Luke Lufkin. I thought my revenge had been sweet, but it really robbed me of any joy. I read somewhere that "Hanging on to revenge is like grasping a hot coal with the intent of throwing it at someone else; you are the one who gets burned."[6] I couldn't help feeling sorry for him then, as that was a pretty mean thing I did. Sooner or later, he'd figure it out and complain to someone who would listen.

Our wonderful, friendly skipper did a complete turn-around after the armistice. He turned into a mean Scrooge-like Dr. Joekyl. When that wet-behind-the-ears ensign put us all on report for too much party, we figured that the skipper, everybody's buddy, would just shrug it off with a wave of his hand. But, oh no! He literally threw the book at all of us. I got a black mark on my permanent record and lost half a month's pay. His attitude was like a change from day to night, and mystified everyone.

"Morale has plummeted to an all-time low," I told my crew one day, and they agreed.

For the next month everybody avoided any unnecessary contact with the "old man," and we sorrowed at the loss of a friend. Then, the rumor filtered down that he was to be transferred to a desk at Navy headquarters and would be losing his sea legs. Some of us could forgive him for taking out his frustrations on us, but some other members of the crew plotted revenge.

Then, we had a change of command ceremony, and a new captain was introduced. He was Robert Leslie, a full commander. He seemed like a real stuffed shirt, but it was really too early for anyone to make an honest appraisal.

Nothing much of any importance ever happens aboard ship without two nerve centers getting wind of it. The wireless shack was one place, and the yeoman's office the other. Between the two of us, we got all the scuttlebutt.

One day Sparks from radio came strutting into my office.

"Pete," he said, "how much will you pay me for the latest scoop?"

"How about a shot of Southern Comfort?" says I.

"You pour, and I'll talk."

He had the most amazing tale to tell. Our new captain, it seemed, had a fetish. He collected teddy bears … and had two trunks full of them stuck all over the walls of his cabin. He had sworn his personal steward to silence, but somehow the information leaked out. The bears were dressed in all sorts of uniforms, some military, some as show people, some as firemen, policemen and postal workers. One was even dressed like a hootchy-cootchy dancer.

"Can you think of any good pranks we can play on him?" he asked, in conclusion.

"Not me," I answered. "At least not until I know that I already have transfer orders out of here…"

Sparks and I did agree that for the time being, we would keep the captain's secret. After all, we wouldn't want to get his cabin steward in trouble.

The situation did, however, provide food for my idle brain… Something to plan and plot for some fun in the future.

We got newspapers and mail every time we came into port and couldn't help but notice how wild the American economy had been.

There was a widespread belief that anyone could get rich in the stock market, and I swore that I would get in on some of the action. Many less affluent Americans were getting into the market and making big bucks.

Investors were buying millions of shares of stock by a new process known as "on margin," a practice similar to buying products on credit. They would pay only a small part of the price and borrow the rest, usually selling the stock at a high enough price to repay the loan and make a profit. It sounded pretty risk free to me, and I couldn't wait for my next shore leave in order to invest one half of my reserve profits.

The other half was going to join up with Bill Creitz and we were going to start selling investment opportunities like stocks in hard-rock mining and oil exploration. Because of their high risk, a higher than normal commission was permitted by law, and we'd planned to add a few other minor fees to that.

It was more a matter of sharp salesmanship than it was value received for amount invested, but people were so money hungry and profit crazy that they'd invest in anything. Now, we didn't intend to really cheat or swindle anyone, but a few little white lies wouldn't hurt. I really needed to get busy and read up some more.

May 30, 1919: We just finished our sixteenth trip to France and this old tub was really in sad need of overhaul. We were loading for our return and expected to be back in New York by June 14th. Our crew (and sometimes passengers) had kept the decks and superstructure clean and well painted, but the hull was a mess. We looked like an old rusty tramp steamer. This bucket never slowed down long enough to clean the hull, and it's too dangerous to attempt it while steaming full-speed at sea.

Since the new skipper came aboard, everybody had to stand watches. Our boatswain had been ill, so I had to help organize and supervise some of the lookouts, so I only got to sleep four hours at a time, and I wrote a little ditty about it:

No fame I crave; before my eye. A simpler goal I keep:
I hope just once, before I die to get sufficient sleep!

My twenty months of scheduled sea duty was more than up, so I was expecting transfer orders when we get back home. Mutt was also expecting a transfer, but Jeff would be staying on with *Huron* for another trip or two. He would be the senior rating left aboard to break in the new chief yeoman, whenever he arrived. Both Mutt and Jeff had been promoted to second-class yeoman's mates and would soon be eligible for first class.

Between them and Sparks, we had the teddy bear "gig" all figured out. When the captain went ashore to report to the admiral, we would get his one dancing bear and hang her from the foremast yardarm with a hangman's noose. Our tailor had fashioned a pair of panties and a brassiere to dress it up in, and just about everybody on the crew was in on it.

We had it timed so that nothing would happen until they got the signal from me. As soon as we docked, a courier should have been waiting with a packet of orders containing transfers for Mutt and me and Alabama Joe, the captain's steward. If the orders were there, it'd been agreed that I would pass the word to "go." But if anyone's orders were missing, we'd have to postpone the joke until another opportunity came along.

U. S. S. *Huron* arrives in New York, June 1919

The big day arrived, on June 13th, we were maneuvered up to our dock in Brooklyn. Arriving a day early, we didn't expect any visitors, like couriers with order packets or replacement men or anybody else. The starboard watch had been given a twelve-hour liberty and I settled down to get some last-minute work caught up.

About three hours into my typing-filing chore, the hatch burst open, and there in my peripheral vision stood the shadow of a man I thought to be a courier and he had a huge stack of transfer orders.

"Don't you usually knock, first?" I growled, not bothering to turn around.

"On your feet, sailor!" It was the admiral!

Pens and papers went flying as I snapped to attention.

"As you were, Yeoman," he replied. "I just dropped this stuff off on my way to the wardroom, because I've got your courier on another errand. Didn't you hear my pipe?"

"No, sir, sorry sir," I stammered.

He told me that he was going up to see the captain and left, and I was left alone, staring at a huge pile of order packets.

A quick shuffle revealed everything we had been hoping for, but I couldn't give the signal to begin "Operation Theresa Bear" until (and only if) the skipper and the admiral left the ship.

My orders were there and I ripped the packet open. "Instructor," they said, "at Y.W.A.S., a school in Kings Point, New York, at the Merchant Marine Headquarters." They were stamped "Effective Immediately." No shore leaves at all! I had no idea where Kings Point could be in New York. Fishing around in my desk, I found my New England atlas and heaved a huge sigh of relief. There it was, only twenty miles from Brooklyn just outside the city on Long Island Sound. It was close enough to see Immy on every liberty! I couldn't have been happier! Oh, joy!

But closer examination of the orders informed me that I was to report at my new billet within six hours of the *Huron's* arrival in Brooklyn, not even enough time to visit Immy for an hour and then only if I could make perfect connections. It was going to be impossible.

What kind of a school? And I turned back to the orders to read some more…

"Yeomanettes?" Did I read that right?

Women in the Navy? It left me to wonder, *What kind of a moron thought this one up?*

But orders were orders, and I had been all packed and ready to go, replacement or not.

About that time, I heard the boatswain pipe the admiral and the captain ashore. So the long-awaited prearranged signal was passed throughout the ship. Jeff would take care of the rest of the orders and I split it down the gangway, seabag in tow. Adios, *Huron*!

I knew it would be dangerous to my career to stick around and see the outcome of our little prank, but I heard it made the big time. A photographer's mate from headquarters came out and got pictures before Captain Leslie returned, and splashed "Lady T. Bear" and her cute undies all over the front page of the *Navy News*. I'll never know, but bet a wooden nickel that Sparks went ashore and called the photographer.

By noon, I was sitting on a hard bench in the Manhattan ferry terminal trying to figure my best route, which appeared to be the elevated and then a horse trolley to Flushing, and at Flushing supposedly catch a Navy bus. There just wouldn't be enough time for the long ride out to Immy's and I felt heartsick.

It was then that I remembered something that had been vaguely nagging me.

"Dunce," I exclaimed out loud, getting hard stares from nearby people. "Sorry," I explained, "I was talking to myself." So saying, I reached into my pocket for a thin packet of letters that had arrived that day. In my haste to launch the Theresa Bear caper, I had forgotten all about them.

A quick shuffle revealed that there was nothing from Immy, but my heart sank when I noticed the only Bronx postmark was from Immy's Mama Gladys. It was a friendly letter, somewhat patronizing and told of her girls making several trips up to the farm for much fun and hayrides with some Bohemian friends.

"Yes, Pete, boy-friends…" the last line read, "I thought you should know."

I certainly felt my heart sinking into the depths of depression. Maybe I should have written more often. I sat on the train mulling over a lot of "What ifs…" And I vowed to make full amends, just as soon as I could. Then, stationed shore-side, I would be able to take liberty almost anytime I wanted, and invest in frequent train rides back to New York. With some of my extra cash, I could even consider buying a car. A three-year-old Model T could be had then for under $250.

King's Point was a small hamlet on the Great Neck Peninsula in Nassau County, southeastern New York, on the northern shore of Long Island, about eighteen miles from South Brooklyn. Less than a mile away was the town of Great Neck with the area's only hotel (more like a small inn) and that's where I would be living, along with three other chief yeoman's mates. We were supposed to teach about fifty young women how to type and process Navy reports. These girls were mostly right out of high school and already knew how to use a typewriter. But we had to teach them the differences between the "right" way, the "wrong" way and the NAVY way to do things. They would be living in a brand-new dormitory, which the Navy just finished constructing. Our classrooms were temporary offices that were no longer needed by some Merchant Marine organization. We had a young lieutenant as our boss, and he was just as big a wolf as we four foxes. Look out, little chicks!

July 11, 1919: What a crazy Navy! They've just turned us "foxes" loose into the chicken house! Oh, joy! This was the kind of a place I had dreamed of visiting ever since I was a kid.

I'd been there for over a month and had seen my Shimmy Immy only once. I telegraphed and wrote her frequently, only to be disappointed when she didn't respond with the same vigor and frequency. I had access to one of these new-fangled telephones through the Navy, but the closest one to her was down at the end of her block.

She was also doing a lot of piano recitals and other performances. I'd been told that her teacher wanted to send her overseas to the Leipzig Conservatory for concert pianists.

We once talked of marriage, but she would have no part of it.

July was a perfect time to explore Long Island beaches. There was a livery stable nearby and I'd been out there a dozen times. Most of the time I took along a different girl.

Some of those beaches were so deserted that you wouldn't see another person for miles, except for one little trollop who loved to remove her bathing shoes and run barefoot in the soft sand. And her feet weren't the only part of her that was bare! I'd seen her three different times and she sure was pretty to look at but so bold she would never let me catch her. She was like a fairy wraith only seen in men's dirty dreams.

I really did love my Shimmy Immy, but I was not cut out to be a hermit, either.

And speaking of foxes turned loose in the chicken house, I wrote another "pome." Its message is clearly one that I could not ignore, by feasting on too many of those "yeomanettes," without getting "stuck."

> *On a moonlit night,*
> *When the moon shone bright,*
> *Two foxes went out for prey.*
> *They trotted along*
> *With frolic and song,*

80

To cheer their weir away.
Thru the woods they went,
But could not scent
A rabbit or a goose astray.
But at length they came
To some better game...
A farmer's barn by the way.
On the roost there sat
Chickens as fat,
As foxes could wish for their dinner.
***

The prowlers soon found
A hole in the ground.
They both went in (the sinners!)
They both went in,
With a squeeze and a grin,
And the chickens were quickly killed;
One of them lunched
And feasted and munched
Till his stomach was nearly filled.
While the other more wise
Looked 'round with both eyes
And would hardly eat anything at all.
"Cunning elf," he said to himself,
"It is plain, the hole is small,
If I eat too much, I'll stick in the wall
And never get out again!"
***

So the matters went on
Till the night was gone
And the farmer came out with a pole.
The foxes both flew,
One of them went thru,
But the greedy one stuck in the hole.
In the hole he stuck,
So full was his pluck

Of chickens he had been eating,
He could not get out,
Or turn about,
And so he was caught by a beating.
***

Sad is this tale
Of the fox's wail,
For the farmer had also a gun.
Poor fox tried to shun,
But to no avail,
And was plastered right in the bun.

#

The only trouble with that duty at Kings Point was that I hadn't been able to figure out how to make any extra money. There was plenty of dough around, though, as quite a few rich celebrities and writers lived nearby. They all had automobiles, so I decided to invest in that Model T that I mentioned earlier. Jeff bought all my surplus booze and smokes so he could keep up our traditions aboard *Huron*. There were no such shortages or quick-buck opportunities landside. But, I'd surely planned to figure something out.

The way that stupid Congress had been leaning, it looked as if whiskey might soon become a scarce item. Earlier in the year, Nebraska had been the thirty-sixth state needed to ratify the constitutional amendment prohibiting the manufacture, sale, transportation or importation of alcoholic drinks in the United States. It was only a matter of time before Congress enacted Prohibition—the Volstead Act—to give effect to that new amendment.

My brain was always churning for ways to beat the system, not only for my own needs, but to make more money. It seemed to me that if the storage of a little booze aboard *Huron* could have produced such a nice profit, a larger hoard would certainly reap a whole lot more. H-m-m?

I had been hoping that Bill Creitz from the black gang would keep in contact, but he got transferred to one of the big cruisers. He had some good ideas for defrauding rich suckers, but I thought that I would be able to figure things out for myself and might be better off working alone, anyway.

I still had most of my shady surplus profits hidden in a bank nearby at a town named Hempstead, and the bank manager over there was named Jacob

Oscale, and he seemed like he might be open to some shady stock investment ideas.

There was this funny feeling somewhere deep in my being, nagging, screaming for release. I thought that I was getting close to a major crossroads of my life and that my millionaire goal was closer on the horizon. I'd have it made if I could connect with Jacob the banker and investment broker. Time would tell.

Chapter 9

Hindu Casks
June 1, 1943

Dear Putzi:

We have been in our new camp for a month but I haven't had time to write before this so I will start at the beginning. We came up the river with a boat load of nurses which I had to guard for some unknown reason from some other unknown. The natives would think twiced before trying to attack most of them Amazon gals. It was quite interesting as we saw some elephinks, and I got quite chummy with the crew when I smoked one of there funny pipes and almost got sick.

They eat rice every meal which they cook in a big brass pot and eat it with there hands. I should say right hand because they told me that the left hand is for something entirely different and is not nice which can't be mentioned in polite literature. They seem to be nice but did not invite me to eat with them, which didn't make me too mad.

After we got off the boat we traveled for some days more on a little dinky train which I could run faster than. Finally one morning we piled off and got on some trucks for a ways and then followed an Indian guide down a path in the jungle and reached our camp.

Well, you should have heard the profane cussing and such because it was not a camp at all but a spot in the jungle where the brush and vines was cut out with a lot of tents piled up in the mud.

So without any breakfast we piled our stuff on the ground and went to work. Some of us raised tents, some of us dug fire pits and straddle trenches, some of us cut wood and finally about 4:00 pm in the afternoon the cooks had boiled water for tea and we had corned beef and hard tacks with it.

Then we had to go back out to the road and carry in our bunks and set them up and then we all took a bath in the chocolate colored river and then went to bed in the dark. From then on it was weary toil every day digging pits and trenches and trying to make the camp livable in the proscribed army manner. For three weeks we had only two meals per day of tea, corned beef and hard tacks but now we have some American canned rations and a little coffee.

We only have Indian cigarettes so most of us took to smoking cigars which we can buy at a bazaar about eight miles away, and now I would trade with anybody for a pack of the once unliked British English cigarettes!

Well, we have had some mail and I got eleven letters from you which were forwarded for our last address in the States. We haven't had time to expect any answers from letters written in this country as the mail here moves by bullock transport which is a cart with big wood wheels that squeak pulled by two denuded bulls, which are something like our steers at home only smaller and with humps on there neck so the Indians can fasten on the yoke which pulls the cart. They drive them with a gode which the first sergeant says is short for go dam you.

We are now settled in our camp but we still live in tents but will soon move into bashas which are made out of baboon trees which are something like sugar cane only bigger and made out of jointed hallowed wood. Over here they just move into a baboon jungle and cut down the big baboons then put up a frame and split the little baboons to weave walls and roof and the whole works with leaves and tie it all together with fibre.

The Indians squat on the ground and cut it up with a big curved sword, which is like a knife. Sometimes in better circles in higher casks the walls are plastered with cow dung which seems to be plentiful everywhere especially in the bazaars at night. But then it is often muddy too so we always don't know what we step in. They should learn there cows to use straddle trenches. But after all the dung is valuable because they mix it with cole dust to make fuel and when they have no cole dust they just make little patty cakes and stack it up to dry in the sun.

Which reminds me, I forgot some other wallas; the carpenter is a baboon-walla, the fuel peddlar is a dung-walla, the flesh peddlar is a nooki-walla and the camp cook for the buffalo-walla is called a chuck-walla!

We are not like all you poor people back in the United States with all those shortages.

We all feel very sorry about all the rationing of stamps. We have plenty to eat here. The potatoes are about the size of peas and speaking of peas we have tots of tea with lots of vitamin P in it but hardly no coffee and no likker except baboon juice which is unhealthy they say. We have delicious chicken, steaks and pork chops all out of the same tin can from Argentina. You half to close your eyes when you eat it. Sometimes we get fruit dates (I mean the kind that grow on trees) and tangerines which are very good. Wild bananas grow in the jungle but are about as big as your pinky and have seeds in them. Awhile back we were issued some live quackers for rations and we have grown so fond of them that they still live as our pet ducks.

Hoping you are the same, I remain

Yours truly, *Gomer Fudd*

#

Hill-billies
June 8, 1943

Dear Putzi:

Can you imagine me setting under a palm tree taking life easy? Well, I tried it once but innumerous anemic leeches attacked me from the rear and besides we haven't any dancing girls here to watch. The only women in this neighborhood are in the road gangs. They usually have a baby on one hip and another one slightly unborn in front, a basket of dirt on there heads, a ring in there nose and an umbrella over the whole works. And when you pass them be sure to do it on the windward side and as many feet away as possible. Thank God for my Esquire calendar else I would forget what real women look like.

One of the boys says we had oughta write home about the flora and fauna of India, but I don't know for sure what that is so will tell you about the hill-billies that come down without any pants on there rear ends. They have big bangs, big knives and goiters around there necks. Also about the monkies we hear howling but hardly ever see and the soldiers we hear griping and see all the time.

We also have long skinny worms about two feet long which make you jump like a snake. We also have snakes with goiters but they are not trained to dance to a flute like the ones we threw Annie and stuff at like I told you onct before. The bugs are too innumerous to mention and I'm glad I'm not a drinking man because even the little pieces of dirt crawl and most of the leaves fly and the leeches get into the queerest places. That reminds me I have written some things about the bugs and the first sergeant who is very educated is going to tell me the Latin scientific names for them so I can tell you all about them. He said he might even help me write some poetry about them. What do you think of my first attempt:

> *This is the land of mystery and romance,*
> *Of ticks and leeches and of flying ants,*
> *Of bugs and cobras and anopheles,*
> *Of much enchanted nonsense, and of fleas.*

#

The birds wake us up here every morning with there singing and it is a good thing because we don't have revelry here and it would be a crying shame to miss breakfast.

We have lots of unusual whether here just like California. That is it rains most of the time although it is supposed to be the dry season. We have a river just back of camp where we bathe and wash our clothes and sometimes the working girls gather on the bank and discuss our good points in Hindustani I guess. They need a little amusement as they only make about twelve Annus per day which is 24 cents American. The men make fourteen Annus and are worth about 2-1/2 cents but some of them are skilled baboon workers and make more. They seen to be happy except when they sing it sounds like they have an awful belly-ake. Some of them are deceased with crickets, which comes from lack of vitamin P. Some also have elephantitus which comes from having an elephink step on you before you reach the age of adultery and some have berry-berry which does not come from cating berries as you would suphose but from eating the wrong kind of rice.

Well, there has been some kind of talk of discharging soldiers who are over 35 so I might see you one of these years. Just now I feel like a grandpa. Hoping you are the same, I remain,

Yours truly, *Gomer Fudd*

P.S. Speaking of the hope of discharge for us older blokes, brings to mind my discharge from the Navy back in the other war. It was the best of times, both good and bad...

#

Bait of Civilian Fate
October 2, 1919

All good things must come to an end, sometimes bitter. This fox visited the hen house one time too many and got caught. As luck would have it, I was making out with one pretty little blonde, when in barged our lieutenant, my boss. It seems that he had designs on the same girl, and whenever a conflict arose between a commissioned officer and an enlisted man, it was not difficult to figure out who would win. He could have made my life miserable, except for the fact that I was heading for a discharge.

Anyway, my time would be up in a couple of weeks and my whole life's drive needed to shift. I had been getting too soft and lazy and the conquest of young yeomanettes no longer held any challenge. It was time now to leave this man's Navy and find new ways to pursue my greater goal of attaining vast wealth.

For reasons unclear to me, BuNav had this dumb requirement that discharged sailors had to return to the town of enlistment before they could receive their final mustering-out pay. Thus it was that three days after I left the Discharge Separation Unit in New Jersey, I was standing on the railroad platform in Minneapolis, trying to remember where the recruitment office was located, so I could get paid. The Navy had paid my train fare to that point, but for the rest of the trip to Iowa, I'd be on my own.

Yes, I'd go back to Ma and Pa in Iowa because I was so close. But, dammit, I'd rather be scheming finance and loving with my Immy in New York. I guessed that a few weeks' delay with family could be tolerated. The train ride from Minneapolis to Strawberry Point was about five hours. I had written to the folks for the first time in a year, requesting someone meet me at the station, so was a little miffed when I exited the train onto an empty platform. *Fine welcome for a war hero,* I thought.

From the local sheriff, I learned that my whole family had packed up and moved to Washington state more than a month before. Pa had found new work in a place called Toppenish, near Yakima.

Damn!

Conscience always plays a part in making any important decision, so having come this far, I knew I'd better continue on west. The unexpected delays were aggravating to say the least. If I had been more faithful about writing letters, I probably could have avoided this conflict.

Damn!

#

As predicted, Congress declared that we would have a liquor drought beginning the next year on January 17th and lasting until the end of time. I thought about buying up some surplus booze, but too many other people had the same idea. Each week we got closer to that black day in January, the cost of liquor doubled. If I hadn't been sidetracked to the Pacific Coast, I'd have a warehouse full of hooch back in New York, but there would be other opportunities.

Ben Franklin said, "A penny saved is a penny earned." To save money, from Iowa I thumbed my way to Washington, taking seven whole days. People didn't travel any distance and sometimes wagons and autos were few and far between. I thought about stealing a horse, but some states still hung horse thieves. Two nights were spent in hobo camps, two nights in haylofts, and two nights in generous farmers' homes, and once in the farmer's daughter. Catching rides and bumming room and board was pretty easy because I still had my uniform and took full advantage of every situation.

The weather had turned wet and cold when I found Ma and Pa. It was like a sad old depressing cinema. Poor Pa had been reduced to finding work processing sugar-beets twelve hours a day in a huge factory. Poor Ma had never fully recovered from that influenza the year before and was still pretty sickly. My older brothers were all back in the Midwest somewhere, except for Frank, who was a preacher and busy with his church. They were living in near poverty and really needed an extra man around the place. My conscience dictated that I stick around for a while to help out. When it came to family, I still had a little moral sense.

All the while helping Ma care for the younger kids, I'd spend time thinking about the prohibition situation, and right off, two opportune thoughts jumped into my head, opening up possibilities. The Canadian border was only a hundred and fifty miles away and gin, vodka and scotch were still available there for a pittance. Smuggling it across the border might offer a challenge, but certainly nothing that a good brain couldn't figure out.

They grew apples there in Toppenish and Pa's cider mill would be working overtime. Also, there are lots of new vineyards popping up around the Yakima Valley. Grape growers in California had been experimenting with a new type of grape jelly called "Vine-go" which, with the addition of water, could make a strong wine within two months. I thought that I may be traveling both north and south in the next few weeks on a fact-finding mission, but in the meantime, I figured that I'd better let Immy know how I was.

#

January 5, 1920
Toppenish, Washington

My Dearest Shimmy Immy;

I received your beautiful Christmas gift and card. Knowing that you care for me is the greatest gift you could give.

We had a joyful Holiday at home with mom and pop and six of my younger siblings. My mamma thinks highly of you and says for me to bring you to Washington so she can meet you. She has high hopes because she keeps your photograph on her mantle and tells all her visiting friends, "That's my Basil's sweetheart in New York and they're going to be getting married."

Pop and I keep telling her to quit pushing, but she just says, "I know what I'm saying, call it a mother's intuition, you'll see!"

It was snowing here in Toppenish, when I arrived last month, and hasn't stopped. What a contrast it is to New York in balmy October, when I got my discharge.

Remember my brother Arthur, who I wrote to you about last November? He wrote mom and said he was planning a business trip to New York next month and would like very much to meet you and your mother. I hope you don't mind if I gave him your address… Play him a beautiful sonata.

I've taken a temporary auditing and accounting job for one of the big fruit packers here in the Yakima valley, but I told them that I planned to return to New York early this year, just as soon as Ma gets to feeling better.

Also, I put my mustering-out pay from the Navy into some choice blue chips stock and have already doubled my money. Let me show you how to invest and make a million. It's so easy when you know how and follow a few "rules."

I'm trying to get it all together and get back to you and New York no later than this time next month. In the meantime, here's how much I miss you:

A long and dismal way I've gone, my dear,
Since that bright radiance of the happy days
You shared with me. The memory of your ways
Is with me still; in ecstasy I hear,
Stealing like music through the lonely air,
The echo of that time, like golden dawn,
That clears my torpid brain, as mists are drawn
From dripping darkness by the sun's first flare.
* * *

A long and dismal way I've still to go,
Before I reach the dusty path of dreams
And walk beside you in the glowing beams
Of love and hope—forgetful of my woe,
Until I'm home at last, and your sweet ways
Dispel the ghosts of all my yesterdays!

Yours with all my love, *Popeye Pete*

#

It took over a year for my mother to fully recover from the ravages of the influenza pandemic. I had tried in vain to get some of my older siblings to share in her care, but they were all too busy making their own way and enjoying marriage and family while I became more and more desperate to get back to my beautiful Immy.

Short trips to Canada and California did help hone my business sense. And I did meet some interesting contacts, but my dream of fortune seemed to be slipping away until one day in mid-1921 Pa told me that he and my sister

Dorothy and young Christian would be able to manage just fine. Ma was much stronger then, so they gave me leave to return to New York, which I promptly did. In time, I brought Ma's prophecy to reality and married my Shimmy Immy.

#

October 5, 1922
Hempstead, New York

Dear Mom and Pop;

Your daughter-in-law, Imogene "Immy" Allaway is a most amazing person. She is so talented, it makes me feel guilty for insisting we marry. She was very reluctant at first, but finally let me talk her into it. She would have preferred instead, to have gone on the stage and been a famous concert pianist.

We married in the Bronx at St. Paul's Lutheran Church. You said you had received the invitation in your last letter. I too am sorry that we couldn't send you the train fare so you could attend. August 5th was a beautiful sunny Saturday, and we went up to Niagara Falls for a four-day honeymoon.

A lot has happened since then, some good, but a lot not so good.

The day we returned from Niagara, Immy was a little disturbed when I told her about a great financial opportunity I had found up in Philadelphia. I should have given her more warning. She was most unhappy that we had to move up there without delay.

She had her job in the dry-goods store, and they assumed that she would be back to work after our honeymoon. More people disappointed!

Immy's mom Gladys and her sisters were a little put out with me too. But, I felt the deal in Philly, although a bit shady, was too good to pass up. By appointment, I met with some people in the Museum of Art, but, I didn't have quite enough cash to swing the deal, so someone else will be making a lot of money, instead of me.

It was a weekend and all the banks were closed. All the cash I owned was in my possession. I left the Philadelphia Museum just after dark and had to walk through Fairmont Park on my way to our new apartment on Hamilton St. I was still stewing about the missed opportunity, when two guys stopped me and asked if I had a light for their smokes. I should have been more wary, instead I fell right into their ploy.

"Sure," I said, and pulled out some matches. Then I was staring into the barrel of a huge old Navy Colt. The scum got $350 in cash, and Grandpa Asa's gold watch, which you gave me for Christmas!

That's not the half of it. When I got back to our apartment, Immy was bawling, and between sobs, told me that we had been robbed while she was out shopping. They got all of our wedding presents and a whole lot more. So much for the "City of Brotherly Love." We had to borrow money to get us back to New York and bum a room from Immy's mother until we could get back on our feet. At least her job at the store was still open.

I do have some good news. Four days ago, I landed a super swell job as bookkeeper for an exclusive woman's sorority named the Colony Club on Park Avenue in downtown Manhattan. I can set my own hours, and once I get their books in order, can probably keep them up in about two days a week.

Immy is very proud of me working for such a prestigious outfit, which is probably the most exclusive upper-crust society for wealthy women in the city. To belong, a woman would have to be one of the famous "400 "families descended from the original colonial families, or married into one, and be registered practically from birth.

We're looking at a house to buy out in Hempstead on Long Island, and I've applied for another job at the Hempstead National Bank. I might have mentioned the manager, Jacob Oscale, in a previous letter. I met him when I was stationed at Kings Point. I'll find out next week if he'll hire me. I'd work for him four days a week and be able to also service the Colony Club with ease.

There are some other high-risk (but very high-return) stocks available in some new mining and oil explorations up here in the Northeast. I'm getting in on the beginning, and am going to build a great business. I've also got the inside track on a couple of promising lobster farms up in Maine and some prime bank securities in Massachusetts. When I work out all the details, I'll be able to make a fortune around the corner from Wall Street.

If you have seen a map of Long Island, Hempstead is 25 miles from Manhattan and is right at the end of the Long Island Commuter Train. I can get into the Colony Club in about an hour and I can walk a short block to the trolley to get to the Hempstead bank.

With the three jobs, we feel we can easily afford the mortgage on our beautiful new home. You would like it very much and if you ever come to New York, we would have a bed for you. It's a two-story, three-bedroom, Dutch-style home, only four years old and has climbing rose trellises on three corners. There is a large yard, and I plan a big garden.

Speaking of gardens, does Pop still have a skunk problem? I wrote a little verse that you both might enjoy:

"BAD-TIME STORY"

Now Poppa's a gonna tall you
A story vot meks you sleep,
A nize vun aboot Rad Ridink Hood,
Or mebbe vun liddle Bo Peep.
Or mebbe vun Peder Rebbet,
Or else der megic trunks ...
Oh no, I know a batter vun
Aboudt der liddle skunks.
Now Mamma Skunk und der children fife
Vere valking in der vood,
Ven all at vunce, my sakes alife!
In front of dem dere stood ...
Tree guesses, liddle mazel toy,
Vot vas standing dere?
'Tvas not a lion, nor yet a volf,
But a great big grizzler bear.
The children said, "Vot shall ve do?"
But Mamma Skunk did say,
In teeney voice so calm und sveet,
"Come children, let us spray."

Until next time, give everyone my love, and wish me luck in all my new adventures; life and marriage are both adventures now, as are my new jobs.

If I've got all my nieces and nephews (your grandchildren) straight, Clyde has four, Lyle two, Frank four, Jeanette five, Agnes seven, Arthur one, and Dorothy three. That makes twenty-six, right? Would you like for Immy and I to give you some more? Write when you can and remember, I'm not going to be moving around any more.

Your Successful Son, *"Popeye Pete"*

Chapter 10

Insecticitis
June 24, 1943

Dear Putzi:

Well, at last I have time to write that letter about bugs. My first sergeant gave me a lot of dope on them including the Latin names for some of them because as I said before he is very educated. He told me of one article he read where a man counted 43,758 lice, 17 ticks and 3 leeches on one holy sadhu while he slept the sleep of the just. A sadhu is just another name for a faker but a faker does not mean a phony like in America, but is a religious fella, maybe called a soul-walla or just-walla.

First I will tell you about the ants. We have some little tiny ones that seem to come out of nowhere and get into our mess kits and on the tables which are officially named *Antis urinea*. Then we have a large red vicious one which parades along wires and clothes lines like so many soldiers which is called the *Antis armyi sovietus*.

But the worst one of all the flying ant that gits in your ears and nose and other orofices with the Latin name of *Termitus pestis goddamem*, which flies around our light at night and finally we half to turn out the light and fire up a candle to roast them with, so while toasting they smell slightly like pork chops and are said to be good to eat. A fella says if you get lost in the jungle you can eat them raw or boiled if you get hungry but he says for us to remove the wings first as they are no good and are hard to chew.

There are lots of different bees here too. One of the boys got stung over the eyes and looked like a Jap for several days and another one got stung on the arm and his arm swelled up twiced as big as your leg—nothing personal, my dear Putzi. I don't know what would happen if someone got stung by one of these local honies.

There are also lots of beetles and one is a tiny thing like a pin head and very brightly colored. There is a rhinoceros beetle with a nasty temper and long pinchers and the armodilla beetle which is four inches long but will curl up into a hard shelled ball when touched. We played catch with one the other day. The buffalo beetle does not resemble the dung beetle of Africa at all, but sure could learn a lesson from it. I still don't know which kind of a beetle the Indians chew. One of the boys said that it grew on trees.

We half to search our bed every night because centipedes get into them and I am sure I would not like to be bit by one of them obnoccuous things.

A very interesting bug of this country is the flying cockroach (*Archy zero pursuitus*) because he is quite timid but will not scuttle like the ordinary kind we have at home (*Archy dirtei sinkus*). Instead of scuttling he will zoom away and I have never been able to catch one.

We have lots of fire flies here too and the first sergeant says that he saw a light in one of the bashas the other night after hours and went down to bawl them out but found that it was only one of them big ones (*Mazda volta amphora*). Three or four of these placed in a bottle would give you enough light to read this scientific letter.

The curse of this place is the leech (*Haemophilia vampiris*). It is an ugly looking worm and you don't feel a thing until you see the blood running down your leg. It spits out some kind of fluid that keeps the blood from clotting and a lot of these attached to your person could be very dangerous. They say the best thing to do when you are in the jungle is to carry a cobra in your pocket and if you start to bleed too much put a little snake venom on the wound and it will clot right now. I don't believe I would like that. One thing they tell us is to never try to pull them off but to touch there butts with a live cigarette, preferably Indian.

The most common Indian insect with the possible exception of the flea (*Mexicani jumpinbeena*) the carrier of blubonic plaque is the common louse (*Cootii shirtus rabbitus*) the carrier of typehus. It is said that the natives do not mind having them as they would half nothing to do if they didn't half to scratch once in a while and life would become very boring.

We have an innumerous number of locusts like grasshoppers but the most interesting is the sawmill variety. How such a little thing can make so dang much noise is beyond me. He will wake you up at night first with a sound like a mechanic filing a saw and then turning on the power while the saw rips through a 30 foot log. There is another one who sets in a tree and grinds his teeth.

There are lots of mosquitoes but the worst one is *Anopheles acrobaticus* which means awful acrobat. He stands on his head but has to stick his long beak into you in order to keep his balance and while doing so he very often gives you the germ of malaria or some other unpleasant nasty decease. If you see one of these standing on his head on your body do not be kind hearted but sock him good!

We have some scorpions that look like dragons and scorpions that look like lobsters and none of them look very good. Likewise the spiders which are sometimes a big as crabs—the water variety. They are very fast but will not bite as a rule unless you try to corner them. Now there are lots of bugs which even the first sergeant does not know the name of. For instance as I sit writing this without a shirt some things like earwigs keep dropping on me from the thatch and they bite too.

So that is about all I know about bugs and the end of this letter. Just from writing it I am starting to feel itchy. Hoping you are the same, I remain,

Yours truly, *Gomer Fudd*

#

Interlude
November 11, 1925

Author's Note: Everything pretty well went "uphill" for Pete after he was discharged from the Navy and married his "Shimmy Immy." They had a beautiful baby girl in November of 1925, who at age four was deeply in love with her daddy. Pete oo-oo-d and goo-ood and played tumble with her, and everybody who saw them together thought that he was the perfect "daddy" and she was the perfect "daddy's little girl."

Dark trouble on the horizon, however, was inevitable, because in the business world, Pete had never fully understood the principle that required him to keep his hands off other people's money.

The reader should observe changes in the style of his prose and poetry now. His outlook will suddenly change from gay, happy and carefree fortune plotting to one of doom and gloom and depression. Here are two samples:

Razors pain you; rivers are damp;
Acids stain you; and drugs will cramp.
Guns aren't lawful; nooses give
Gas smells awful; so I'll try to live.

And then, he offers some good advice, but too little, too late:

Lady, lady, should you meet
One whose ways are all discreet,
One who murmurs that his wife
Is the loadstar of his life,
One who keeps assuring you
That he never was untrue,
Never loved another one.
Lady, lady, better run!

The stories continue ...

Chapter 11

Tokyo Rose
July 3, 1943

Dear Putzi:

I just received your letter so I will now take typewriter in hand and pen you another line or two from Hindustan and tell you all the dope, officious and otherwise, about our present situation. So your brother is now a G.I. Well, I hope he finds things as interesting in his camp as I have everywhere.

Or to put it in better English I hope he can adopt himself to the new life and take the aversities of fate with a grin. As I sorta incindered before I have been working very hard expecially since last week when we had a confliguration which burned up our administration basha and a lot of our stuff.

Just a few days before we had received kits free gratis from the United States which contained athalitic equipment, radio, and so forth. We were all setting around with the radio playing in our working clothes, telling antidotes, kidding one another and blessing Madame Curie for discovering the radio when someone hollered fire and we didn't have time to save hardly nothing. So the next morning we all had to take the bull by the tail and look the proposition in the face and so that is why I have been working so hard.

We saved the radio but we can only get Tokyo and half to listen to their thinly veiled insinuendoes about the United States being too yellow to fight, and so forth. But of course we all know better and take any statement of the Japs with a dose of Tokyo Rose salts.

We all get along pretty good of course this is no young ladies semetary and the talk and manners are not quite kosher YMCA but we half learned to look over the faults of the other fellas and we never half had any violent alternations in spite of living in such close quarters.

Although we have had a few accidents in our work we have had very little sickness. They preach about malaria prevention all the time and I certainly don't want to catch it as I had it twice when I was younger. The last time was in bed with a private nurse but she couldn't seem to do me any good for a week or more.

Some of the boys have dobie itch. In the States a dobie is a kind of mud they use to build houses with in Arizona and New Mexico but over here it is a fella that does your washing except according to there rules he should be called a wash walla which I could never savvy why they call him dobie instead. The itch is caused by the dobie laying your clothes on the ground to dry and a fungus gets into them so you get athaletic feet all over your body. Knock wood, but I haven't had anything since I was indicted into the surface except having some new china store teeth put in.

Now that the whether is getting real hot we are bothered some around camp by obnoccuous reptiles and the insects are also getting worse. Speaking of the latter the natives in the bazaars around here burn some kind of insects in little lamps and it smells real nice.

There is not much to see around here sometimes we have a group of monkies on the other side of the river too. Last month five buffalos came through the camp and they look very sad. Otherwise there are only goats blatting around little humped backed cows chewing there cubs and once in a while we see a bunch of vultures setting around a caucus in fragrant delicto as the Roman poet Ibid says, Oh, death where is thy stink?

In the bazaars sometimes you will see a devoit Muslim squatting down reading the Kodak or a painted proselyte plying her ancient and immortal profession. In the larger places you will sometimes see a fat, pompous and oboese overweight Indian riding around in a jigsaw pulled by a coolie.

In the United States the Indian squabs carry there porpoises on there back as you know but over here they carry them astraddle of there hips. The women mostly dress the same all alike. It would not be hard for a girl to get her torso ready for a wedding. Just buy some yard of goods and wrap it around in the proscribed manner.

Most of the people are poor because they are too insolent to work. Very few of them are direct and when you ask them something they give you an amphibeous answer or they say No Engleesh. They say that lots of people over here can't read or write and are illustrate.

It seems a shame that men and women can't get married before bearing children expecially when there are some who go too far and commit bigotry but then they are mostly the rich. On the other hand some of these people are very poor and all they half is at the front. Well anyhow as Mr. Herbert Hoover used to say Posterity is just around the corner.

How is the war coming over there? All we hear is the Japanese side of it which sounds like the fables of Aesophagus. To hear them talk they will take over the world like Kotex conquered the Axtecks in Mexico. Well, they can never do it. There idea that everybody should take a new order with castor oil if necessary will never win over the democratic idea that a man does what he sees fit and sees to it that everybody else does the same.

One Saturday, our kind old sergeant showed up with a gharry-walla and some kind of a secret contrabund under a trampolin. The gharry-walla stood around crying, "Buckshee, buckshee," with his hands out. Then the sarg says to pay the man everybody because you're going to like what he's got hidden under the trampolin. So, we passed the helmet and collected more than in church. And would you believe it? His cart was loaded! I mean to say loaded with warm English-British beer, so we all got loaded too. Oh boy!

Well, I must go jump in the river as I am feeling hot, sticky and very crummy. Hopeing you are the same,

Yours truly, *Gomer Fudd*

P. S. Speaking about getting loaded, you know just after the last war, we had Prohibition which meant no likker or beer at all. And this reminds me about those hard times…

#

London Bridge Is Crashing Down

October 22, 1929: I had never known such prosperity! It seemed that my middle name must have been Midas and everything I touched turned to gold. Most stocks were so hot then, that many investors were doubling their money in less than a year, and some in only four months.

Bill Creitz, who used to be a stoker in the black gang aboard *Huron*, wrote me a couple of years before, telling me to contact a friend of his who had a great deal on lobster farm stock up in Maine. Maybe I mentioned it earlier. There were a couple of other "under-the-table" investments that we handled. Bill's friend supplied me with contracts and stock certificates and we divvied up the proceeds. I wouldn't sell to anyone where I was known, but drove my Model T over to the south side of the island, for a little door-to-door salesmanship one or two days a month. A lot of rich, elderly widows lived over around Freeport and Merrick, and I did pretty good down there. Sooner or later those old broads were going to get wise, so I had to be careful. When that field ran dry, I could always go back to the Kings Point village of rich celebrities and authors.

The year before, the Revenuers rounded up and arrested more than 75,000 people for violation of Volstead's Prohibition. Creitz and I thought we were still safe because we restricted entry to our speakeasy to very limited friends.

I guess I never mentioned how easy it was to set that venture up. We had never purchased any illegal hooch, so they couldn't trace us that way. The dummies were still trying to figure out what happened to a warehouse full of booze back in 1924. We had enough stockpile left yet to last at least until 1933. If anything happened to either one of us, the other would get sole ownership. It wasn't the most profitable venture because we had to support such a large team of security guys.

I was such a matter-of-fact crook! I should never have written any of this stuff down, but nobody will ever read it anyway.

At the bank, I proposed a deal to Jacob, about how we could "borrow" some of the bank's money for a short time, and invest it in some real money making blue chips. I could "cook the books" to hide the shortage, until we made our profit, and then return the original amount. I figured that he would go along and he did. We figured five grand if properly invested, would almost double in a year. Well, we took the plunge and we'd made over $6,000 profit on paper, so we planned on cashing out the stocks and returning the money a couple of weeks later.

Immy couldn't believe that we almost had our house paid off, and as soon as we did that, I promised to take her on a steamship cruise to Paris. She quit her job and in between concert recitals, was now a full-time mom for our little girl, who was almost four.

I only went into Manhattan to the Colony Club for five hours on Saturdays, plus one full day once a month. They didn't pay very much, but I had a double-dipping scheme there too, if you know what I mean. I should say "triple-dipping" because some of those younger society matrons had been so hungry for love, they'd Purr-r-r any way they could get it.

One in particular came on to me so strong that I just had to get her to bed. We cooked up the story that she was an investment broker and that we had to attend a two-day business seminar in Boston. I asked Immy if she would sit the three-year-old son of the woman for the weekend, to which she readily agreed. Immy and I weren't getting along like we used to, and I thought she would get suspicious, but she was so trusting and so innocent.

Every day the market gained, and we made more money. I knew it was risky to leave it all in one basket (as my Ma used to say), but just a day or two more and it would yield a couple of more bucks!

NEITHER BLOODY NOR BOWED

They say to me, and so they should,
It's doubtful if I come to good.
I see acquaintances and friends
Accumulating dividends,
And making enviable names
In science, art and parlor games,
But I, despite expert advice,
Keep doing things I think are nice,
And though to good I never come ...
Inseparable, my nose and thumb!

#

Easy come, easy go! The world had crashed around me! Stock prices reached their height in September 1929. People invested billions of dollars in the stock market, obtaining money by borrowing from banks, mortgaging their homes, and selling lower-risk government securities.

Buying stock on margin (with someone else's money) was a risky bet that the price of that stock would continue to increase. But, the market didn't increase and some smarter investors began selling, and as they sold it caused a decline in prices, which in turn especially threatened all of us who had purchased on margin.

On October 29th the New York Stock Exchange, the largest in the world, had its worst day of panic selling. By the end of the day stock values had declined by $10 billion to $15 billion.

The month before it had been my baby girl's birthday, and I had to pawn Immy's diamond engagement ring in order to buy my daughter a nice birthday present and a party. But before we could get the party started, two plain-clothes coppers came to the door. I thought for sure they were from the federal government, but instead they informed me that Jacob Oscale had been arrested and that I was next. He was my boss, the manager at the bank, you remember. All the money we had jointly "borrowed" from the bank had been lost in the stock market crash.

The coppers said that they had to take me in for embezzling money from my bank. As they walked me up the street to their car, we paused and I looked back to wave at my little girl and my wife, who were peering sadly out the window. I will never forget the tugging sorrow I felt in my heart.

I spent the first two nights in the Suffolk County Jail twenty-five miles from home. Then they took me before a judge in Brooklyn. Jacob and I had taken almost twelve grand, and we were charged with the theft of $5,992 each. Neither of us had any resources for bail, so we spent another week in the Kings County Jail until trial could be set. We could have gotten away with this if the damned government hadn't forced a "bank holiday" to slow down the money run. It was only because of that, the auditors discovered our little scheme.

To make matters worse, Bill Creitz came by my cell one day for a visit.

"When our 'protectors' heard you got busted," he informed me, "they trucked off with all our booze. And I've no idea where." He looked real sad, almost like an actor, overacting.

I didn't know whether to believe him or not. He could easily be in on the deal and knew exactly where our stock had been moved. But, there in the pokey, there wasn't anything I could do to challenge the lying sonofabitch.

The U. S. District Court in Brooklyn indicted me, but I pled guilty in order to avoid a trial. I was now a felon, but the court was lenient, stating they would suspend my sentence, if I could replace the money.

It was hard, but by re-mortgaging our house, selling my little car and cleaning out Immy's saving account, I was able to avoid long-term jail time. With no job at the bank now, I would have to rely more on other ventures, including a little deeper dipping at the Colony Club. Some of those rich old widows were easy prey for donations to some fake charity, using company names which Bill Creitz's friend printed up. Everybody who could was willing to help out disabled children and some World War widows and orphans, or so they thought.

Immy knew that I had hocked her diamond ring, but she didn't know that I'd replaced the diamond with glass. She also was unaware that I'd spent all of her savings, and now I had to tell her that I'd had to re-mortgage the house. She was not going to be happy with me, and I really felt like a heel!

For you alone, I write this verse,
I know my style could not be worse,
But in this versifying mood
I try to bring an interlude
For you, sweetheart, from things adverse.
***
In all this dreary universe,
There's no man who could reimburse
To offer their solicitude,
For you alone.
***
I wish that I could but disperse
The Cares and troubles that immerse
Your mind each day, and then intrude
With gifts, into your solitude;
My bursting heart, and empty purse,
For you alone.

Maybe I should have listened more to my good ol' Mama. What a mess of things I'd made, a fine kettle of fish!

\#

Oh, lead me to a quiet cell
Where never footfall rankles,
And bar the window passing well,
And gyve my wrists and ankles.
Oh, wrap my eyes with linen fair
With hempen cord go bind me,
And in your mercy, leave me there,
Nor tell them where to find me.

Oh, lock the portals as you go,
And see the bolts be double,
Come back in half an hour or so
And I will be in trouble!
Oh, seek my love, your newer way;
I'll not be left in sorrow,
So long as I have yesterday,
Go take your damned tomorrow!

Chapter 12

Jungle Boredom
July 28, 1943

Dear Putzi;
Well, it is getting very dull around here. The senser won't allow us to tell you what we are doing for the war effart so instead I'll tell you that we have built and furnished a nice little recreation basha. We even have a bar and one of the boys put up a sign that says Hope springs eternal. We are trying to think up a name for our club. Some of the suggestions are Inn of the Flying Bull, Bore's Nest, ecsetera.

If things get any more stagnant around here I am going to go on a good bust one of these days and I don't mean the kind you ladies wear and drink until I fall into a comma. One of the boys says it would help if there was a few *Hors de combat* around here. That is French and means lady camp followers. Ye gads, but I sure do miss my little Putzi!

I'm now editor of the Company's new newspaper, called *The Tiger Rag* but as there is no other news I must fall back on my lectures about India. Last night we killed a snake six feet four inches long. I don't know what his name was. This morning I spent some time watching the jungle in which the hand of man has apparently never set foot. There are lots of flowers if a man could brave the snakes and so forth. A fella could gather corteges of orchids and gardenias for his best girl with no trouble at all. I am glad I haven't any close by around here as I might be bit by something unpleasant just thinking about you. We have been warned not to catch the monkies as some of them have rabbis but there is no harm in watching them imitate Tarzan or do there anesthetic dancing on top of a huge tree.

Well, last week I saw an Indian wedding. They have a long procession with a fella beating on a large tum tum at the head of it. All the principals wear bright yellow sarees and instead of going bear foot they wear scandals on there feet.

A saree is just a long strip of cloth made from safflowers which they wind around something like a togo. I haven't learned much about marriage yet.

In the old days the natives use to practice suttee but the British English made them quit because it made too much smell. Suttee is not something you sit on but is a big pile of wood set on fire with a dead corps on top and his wife that is not dead. That must have been rather painful, don't you think?

We half fixed our camp up very nice. We have had a gang of coolies working here for some time Some of them work very well but sometimes you feel like kicking them because they are so obstinate in the seat of there pants only as I said before they don't wear any hardly. They have cleared spaces in front of each basha and made little rock gardens and planted ferns and banana trees. We also have floored our bashas and have screened the doors and windows and have the best camp for miles around. Of course we wouldn't have except that Alibi and his forty thieves belong to this company. Now we can sit in comfort each evening after we squirt a lot of infanticide around to kill the pets.

Well dear keep on writing those nice letters. Of all the fast friends I have made in my life you are one of the fastest and I certainly appreciate it. So now I must quit and go to work although I am too hot to be of any use. Hoping you are the same, I remain

Yours truly, *Gomer Fudd*

P. S. Speaking of going to work, one morning after the last war, I went to work at a place called the Colony Club, and that day my life was changed forever…

#

A Cowardly Fugitive
March 25, 1930

Dearest Shimmy Immy;

Oh, how I've dreaded the possibility of this day coming! To my sorrow, it has arrived!

Be strong, my love, as I know you have the inner strength to survive the coming struggle. I only wish that I could tell our sweet little princess how much I love her, but I will have to count on you to do that for me.

I've done some bad things, some you know about, but not all, and I'm going to have to go away for a while and change my name.

I'm too great a coward to be able to face a long prison term, and you have every right to know the reasons:

When I kissed you both good-bye this morning, who could possibly have known it would be our last… When I got to the Colony Club to start work, I stopped to have a smoke with the doorman.

"Some auditors are in there checking the books," he said, "and they have been asking for you, and old lady Hearst has been sobbing all morning."

A chill ran down my spine and I started to turn away, telling him, "I'll be right back, I forgot to buy my newspaper."

As I walked away, he hollered after me, "Hey, Pete, you're not in any kind of trouble, are you?"

I never saw the man again, but I'm sure he got his question answered later that day.

Please don't hate me, my darling, but you must know that by me running, they will have no claim on you. I'm not sure how much I stole from the Colony Club because it was in little dribs and drabs; a hundred here, five hundred there. Every cent has been spent or was lost on the stock market, and there is no way that I can pay this one back, so I must flee.

I just wish I could see that snooty Mrs. Hearst's face when the whole story hits the newspapers. The scandal will destroy her, because the Club always kept such a low profile that few people even knew it existed, and they abhor publicity of any kind, even good.

I'm sure the coppers will come by, looking for me, but if I don't tell you where I've gone, you can't tell them. Give my little princess a hug.

You look at me as if you thought
That I was quite insane,
And all this work is done for naught
Except to clear my brain.
You know, my brain is full of fleas,
There's dandruff in my hair
But still I try so hard to please,
And end that doubting stare.

With sadness, I say Good-bye, *Popeye Pete*

#

May 21, 1931: It was fourteen months until I next had anything noteworthy enough to write about. I had changed my name and was now using an alias of John Joseph Bart. Only one other person besides myself in Portland, Oregon knew who I really was.

Two days after I left New York, in March, they published the results of the audit of the Colony Club and could not account for between $10,000 and $11,000, which seemed about right to me. The *New York Times* reported on April 13, 1930, that I had been indicted (in absentia) by the King County Grand Jury in Brooklyn and that a nationwide search had begun. I suppose that was what the modern police people called "an all-points bulletin (APB)."

On that day, I was in Minneapolis and just found out that my brother Arthur had moved out of there eleven years earlier. What a surprise! I guessed that if I had written home more often, I'd know more about what was going on... but there's no way I could let my frail mama know what a crook I was. I just hoped that the coppers didn't have any information on my family and origins. I was pretty sure that I could "get lost" in the Pacific Northwest. But first, I took a train down to New Orleans to see my brother Hillary.

I had a good reason to be using an alias, but he wouldn't tell me why he was telling everyone that he was a prize fighter under the alias of "Charles O'Keefe," and that he had been born in Ireland.

"What'd you do, Hillary," I asked, "hold up a bank, or what?" He turned a bright shade and wouldn't talk to me at all about it, which led me to believe that he was also a fugitive from the law, like me.

I stayed with him and his wife Ann in New Orleans for about a week, and bought a used car, and then drove to Portland. There, I looked up my old shipmate, William (Bill) Creitz, and entered into a partnership buying and selling business opportunities. He still insisted that he had lost his shirt like me when all our booze had been stolen.

I was having second thoughts about some of the company that I was keeping ... everybody drank too much booze and I was getting to the place where I couldn't go without it, either. Prohibition was still going strong, but there was talk of repeal because booze flowed so freely and could be obtained almost anywhere. I heard the feds were getting discouraged and giving up.

I was living then in a cheap hotel (almost a flop-house) in uptown Portland, just over a Chinese restaurant. I had a room on the fourth floor and had to walk up the stairs because the elevator was broken most of the time. Six days out of seven, my only companion was a couple of bottles.

If I hadn't been a wanted fugitive, I might have lived in a better place and not be looking over my shoulder all the time. I didn't know how much longer I could take that running away. Every knock on the door was imagined to be a dreaded investigator…

Once upon a midnight dreary, while I guzzled, tight and bleary
Out of many falsely labeled bottles of intoxicator
While I nodded, nearly sleeping, suddenly I felt a-creeping
As if one was slyly peeping, peeping through my ventilator,
"'Tis some dry investigator peeping through my ventilator,
Just some dry investigator."
***
Quite distinctly I remember, With my hate's bright glowing ember,
How I longed to quite dismember that sweet young prevaricator.
Eagerly I wished the morrow; vainly I had sought to borrow
From my gin surcease of sorrow, but my sorrow was the greater
For that devilish female baiter, for that false and fickle dater,
Holy Moses, how I hate her!
***
As I sat and drank my liquor, suddenly there came a snicker
And a sound of rustling quicker than a hurried hash-house waiter;
So that now, to still the beating of my heart, I stood repeating
"'Tis some visitor entreating entrance at my ventilator,
Some late visitor entreating entrance at my ventilator;
It is late, but they've come later!"
***
Presently my soul grew stronger; hesitating then no longer,
"Who the hell is that who's prowling like a sly assassinator.
Go away, for I am sleeping, and I hate your belly creeping,
Never let me catch you peeping, peeping through my ventilator."
Then I thought of my fair baiter, so I oped the ventilator,
Nothing there to indicate her.

* * *

Back into my chamber turning, all my soul within me burning,
And I felt a sudden yearning, and I wondered if I hate her.
To my door I turned back at, there a sly and grinning black cat
Entered through my ventilator, like a creeping alligator,
Perched upon my radiator, like a leering alligator,
'Twas that damned intoxicator.

* * *

In his eye I read a warning, that I'd live to rue the morning,
And awake to find her scorning my true love that seems to sate her.
In my ire, I threw a flask at the grinning, leering mask
Of the slick and slimy cat perched upon my radiator
But the damned intimidator, only sat up all the straighter,
Croaked the words, "Aw, you don't hate her!"

* * *

From the cat this caught me blinking, and in fear I started shrinking,
And my mind was wildly thinking, wondering if I really hate her,
Hearing such a ghastly earful, I just shuddered somewhat fearful,
And my thoughts were far from cheerful gazing at this dreadful baiter,
At this cat or alligator, at this spooky aggravator
Perched upon my radiator.

* * *

Then I felt my pulses quicken, as I sat there dumbly stricken
Till my soul began to sicken, and that damned intoxicator
Made me shaky in the liver, made my arms and legs to quiver
Made the sweat run like a river while that grim and awful baiter
Puffed and seemed to grow much greater, sitting on my radiator,
Growled again, "Now, do you hate her?"

* * *

Terrified, I hoped 'twas dreaming, tried to call but vainly, seeming
I had lost my power of screaming, paralyzed by that dread baiter,
In my fright, I must have fainted, for the morning sunlight painted
Scenes of beauty quite untainted by a slimy alligator,
Nothing on my radiator, nothing on my ventilator,
And, I knew I didn't hate her.

* * *

Soon I heard a gentle snoring, turned around and then adoring
My fair one, and God imploring sense to be a dream translator,
Seemed to hear the answer slow, "Read no more of Edgar Poe,
He's an old prevaricator; there are lots of writers greater."
Then I snuggled closer to her, knowing that my love was greater,
Knowing I could never hate her.

Never try to associate "her" in any of my verse, with a real person. By way of interpretation, "her" in the above was only my appetite for alcohol, a "lover" that I kept trying to hate.

Bill Creitz and I were doing pretty good, and I would soon be able to move out of that fleabag to a much nicer apartment. I'd also taken a job as traveling auditor for Farmer's National Grain Corporation. There were lots of nice ladies out there in the farm-lands of Oregon and Washington, but I met one down at Eugene who I really like a lot, named Angeline. She was going to the University of Oregon and lived over in Idaho.

My expense account from Farmer's allowed frequent overnight lodging when I was away from Portland. Downtown hotels were okay, but I preferred checking into the new motor courts under the shade of a huge cottonwood tree.

I wooed Angeline with a new poem:

IMMORTAL EYES,
I dream of them each night,
They grow like stars from dark till morning light,
They fill my dreams with ever-burning fire,
And keep me chained forever, and inspire
Stuff like this verse, when I'm not even tight!
***

No doubt, my dear, you think my verses trite
When I rave on, and all your charms recite,
But though you doubt them, you should still admire
IMMORTAL LIES!
***

If I were real poetic, and could write
Of love and bliss and glowing, pale moonlight
In flowing hand, and not sit and perspire,

Trying to pluck the dead strings of my lyre,
If I could do this, then your charms I might
IMMORTALIZE!

I grieved sometimes for the rotten deal I caused my first family. I often looked for justification, but found none. I might even (mis-) quote some Scripture from Mark 10:29, which said, *"...there is no man that hath left house, or brethren, or sisters, or father, or mother, or wife, or children, or lands ... but he shall receive an hundredfold now in this time, houses and brethren, and sisters, and mothers, and children, and lands..."*

In October 1930, I almost lost my job with Farmer's because I spent nine days in the Multnomah County Jail for signing some partnership checks without sufficient funds. It worried me for a while that somebody might make a connection with the New York wanted posters, but it never happened.

I thought that it was time to break my partnership with Bill Creitz, and to try going straight for a while.

In December, Angeline had some harsh words with her parents and left home and moved to Portland. She took a job with a life insurance company. We were both looking for something and found each other. She did not like her name, and wanted to be called "Jerry."

Then, in May 1931, Jerry and I got married. Oh, joy!

June 20, 1932: Oh, boy! I was papa again to a hefty baby boy. He was born to my precious Jerry this morning at 3:00 a.m. We named him Rodney. I really loved this family life and was trying so hard to live by the straight and narrow.

Angelina Martino lived in Idaho,
That sounds like a wop, but she wasn't, y'know,
She had all the beauty that God could bestow!
(And that's going some.)
***

Giacoma Guisseppe Bartisti, by trade
A poet who lived in New York, unafraid,
He wanted to wonder, but right there he stayed.
(The poor sap!)
***

Angelina Martino and Bartisti too,
Both looked for someone who was loving and true,

But love at long distance they neither could do.
(It ain't natural.)
***

So they lived and flirted quite merrily,
They couldn't have loved each other, y'see
For to love, one needs some proximity ...
(Hence my title)
***

But that they should love the Fates did portend
They each went on journeys their spirits to mend
And both met in Portland, and that is the end!
(Ain't you glad?)

No more crooked life for me, I finally had a little family and I loved them dearly, I had a good-paying job and everything was going to turn out okay. I was even going to try giving up the booze. The only ghostly shadows from my past were the wanted posters from New York and the giving up of my family name. I couldn't contact Mama or any of my siblings, without risk. Those New York coppers were too damned persistent. So for the rest of my life, I supposed that I'd be John Joseph Bart (alias *Guisseppe Bartisti*).

Chapter 13

Calcutta
September 11, 1943

Dear Putzi:

A lot has happened since I wrote my last missile. I am in Calcutta now and can tell you where I have been because it is all in the newspapers. I have been up in northern Assam and Burma building the Ledo Road. Just before I left we took a trip as far as we could go and believe me there are some mountains. In some places it is so far down it takes you over a half-hour just to see the bottom. Here's what the paper had to say:

THE LEDO ROAD

The curtain of secrecy was partially lifted this week from the building of the Ledo Road which since December 14 of last year, has been pushed tediously from Assam in eastern India across the thickly-jungled northern Burma border. Friendly advisers informed (all commanders) that the grandiose S.O.S. task "couldn't be done." But in spite of monsoon weather which spills from 200 to 300 feet of water a year, in spite of tenacious jungle, in spite of what is described as the worst malaria country in the world and in spite of Japanese opposition, the road has snaked its way inexorably toward the old Burma Road, with which it may someday link. With tools ranging from crude picks to huge bulldozers, rugged white and Negro American Engineer troops, Chinese engineers and slim Indian laborers have fought all difficulties with a tenacity that has met and defeated the odds stacked against them...The road has been well protected from air assault by the U.S. Air Force. When the project is completed, it may be a partial answer to supplying the Chinese in their struggle against the Jap invader.[7]

Two other articles of interest from the same paper were:

NEW YORK—(AP)—Metropolitan policewomen were given a combination pistol and make-up kit known as a "gruesome twosome" or "lady cops carryall."

The kit is pigeonholed to avoid the dangers of pulling out lipstick when reaching for the gun. It is eight inches square, with a center pocket for a colt automatic. Next to the Colt are powder, rouge and lipstick, covered by a flap.

One lady cop commented: "The lipstick is as necessary as the gun when you are trapping a masher and a lady cop ought to have all her weapons handy."

and:

The New York Yankees had a vestige of power last year with Keller and DiMaggio in the outfield, but Joltin' Joe traded his bat for a bayonet. On the other side of this year's World Series, Alpha Brazle, brilliant rookie southpaw pitching ace for the St. Louis Cardinals, has been ordered to report next week for induction into the Army.

Brazle, winner of seven games in eight tries, expects to be able to re-join his mates on furlough in time to play in the World Series against New York.

I suppose you wonder what I am doing here in Calcutta. Well, I got my orders to go home but don't know when I leave. We are housed and live in a place with a fancy name called Tulsi Mansions but it is not so fancy. We half to walk up six flights and sleep on the same old charpoys. I guess I didn't tell you what a charpoy is. Well, it is a wood frame with a heavy cord stretched across kitty corner. No matter how many blankets you fold under you still look like a waffle in the morning. I am supposed to be working out in a warehouse at Kidderpore but I am now engaged in playing hookey which nobody cares about.

There was some good news waiting when we arrived here and that was that the Eyeties of Italy have been knocked out of the war. Marshall Baggadolio surrendered to General Eisenhower three days ago on September 8th but all the Nazi troops were ordered to stay in Italy. That might mean another battleground. I'm sure glad that I'm headed home.

It took us six and a half days to reach here from the jungle and we saw lots of sad sights with people dying all around from the famine that is now going on at this place. You cannot share your food with the people as they would rather die than eat gentile food like meat and stuff like we eat. They only eat rice and there is no rice because the crop was poor. So they sit on the sidewalk and starve while cows are wandering all over the place.

Yesterday's *Hindusthan Standard*, a British newspaper for Friday, September 10th had back page headlines like: "182 Bodies Picked Up In Streets In A Week" and on another page: "992 Starving Persons Being Treated In Hospitals."

Those wandering cows keep tying up traffic, which is mostly jigsaws. I rode in one but I felt sorry for the poor fella pulling me and so I mostly walk to wherever I'm going to. Maybe he was a saw-walla.

We have met some nice British-English soldiers. One of them invited us to the home of a very old lady relative for dinner. She has a beautiful home with servants all over the place and we enjoyed ourself.

We have a pretty nice club here called the Red Cross club and we go there to eat sometimes. There was a dance on Sunday night but I did not dance as I was too bashful and most of the girls were very young and a lot of them were very black also. I met a Red Cross girl called Peggy who is also going home she says.

Well, I have not heard any news yet but I am getting very anxious. Hoping you are the same, I remain

Yours truly, *Gomer Fudd*

P.S. While I am waiting so anxiously to get home to you, I am reminded of that other time in 1932 when my home was the "Big House," scheduled for ten years, and I had lost all hope of ever getting home again…

#

Alphonse Capone's Sing Sing
November 11, 1932

November 11, 1932: When I got to the "big house," they took everything away from me. But I still had my memories. I arrived there on Armistice Day, the anniversary of when the World War ended. Back then was that time in my life when I was still innocent. Perhaps I was a little crooked, but it was not yet too late to have changed my ways.

That day was also my daughter's birthday. I wondered if she still remembered her daddy? I wondered what dear Immy had told her about me? What a heel I'd been to both of my lovely children!

So there I was in Sing-Sing Prison at Ossining, New York, facing down a ten-year sentence. Oh, woe was me! My next-door cellmate was the notorious Alphonse "Scar-face" Capone, who masterminded the Chicago gangland killing known as the Valentine's Day Massacre.

What a fool I had been to think that I could have escaped the long arm of the law. What made me boil was that the fickle finger of fate waited until I had honestly decided to go straight, and then tripped me up.

It had been an innocent thing that did it; I was involved in a minor auto accident with a guy named A. W. Stevens at Milwaukie and Claybourne Streets in Portland. It had been a minor fender bumper, not causing much damage, and we had exchanged names and settled up the damages between us. That should have been the end of it, but Mr. Stevens had too good of a memory for faces and he also liked to read *True Detectives Mysteries* magazine.

A couple of months earlier, the magazine had published a big spread about the Colony Club theft and a photograph of some guy named Basil Allaway who was a missing fugitive from New York. Now, I'd always wanted to have my picture in the papers, but not like that. They'd offered a reward of $350 to anyone who could help solve the mystery, and Stevens jumped at his chance.

Coppers were at my door early the very next day. They woke my two-month-old son and terrified my little Jerry. I remembered it was August 16th, because I had an appointment with my boss that morning to talk about a raise.

We had no chance to say good-bye because they nabbed me the moment I answered the door, wearing only bathrobe and slippers.

They were a lot rougher with me this time, clamping on leg irons first thing. I got to see a judge that first day still dressed in only bathrobe and slippers, but I knew the jig was up and waived extradition. Somewhere in the jail, they found me some clothes. And I could hear my poor Jerry wailing and full of questions somewhere down the labyrinth of hallways.

"Can't I see her for just a minute or two?" I pleaded.

"Not on your life, Bartisti, or whatever your name is," sneered one officer. "We're not taking any chances on losing you again."

They had me on a train to New York within forty-eight hours. It was quick and dirty; after standing in a lineup for positive identification. Later, in the courtroom, I pled the only way I could; "guilty!" And I could hear haughty old Mrs. Hearst, who threw enough tirades at me that the judge had to order her out of the room.

Then I sat in the New York City jail for five long weeks until Judge Levine[8] could find five minutes' time on his calendar to haul me in and tell me, "Ten years!"

Ossining was a village in Westchester County, north of New York City, on the eastern bank of the Hudson River. The village used to be known as Sing-Sing, for the Sin Sinck native peoples, from 1813 to 1901, when the name of the village was changed to Ossining to avoid identification with Sing-Sing Prison that opened in 1825.

#

I do not like my state of mind;
I'm bitter, querulous, unkind.
I hate my legs, I hate my hands,
I do not yearn for lovelier lands.
I dread the dawn's recurrent light;
I hate to go to bed at night.
I snoot at simple, earnest folk,
I cannot take the gentlest joke.
I find my peace in paint or type,
My world is but a lot of tripe.

I'm disillusioned, empty-breasted,
For what I think, I'd be arrested.
I am not sick, I am not well
My quondam dreams are shot to hell.
My soul is crushed, my spirits sore;
I do not like me, any more.
I cavil, quarrel, grumble, grouse,
I ponder on the narrow house.
I shudder at the thought of men...
Who chain me to the wall again.

Add to that sorrow then, the fact that Prohibition had finally ended just as I landed in there. Oh! Could I really have used a drink! And, damn that fickle finger of fate!

#

Spring, 1933:

My dear Jerry;

Thank you for sending me your new address in Oakland, California. It's nice that your insurance company employer is so accommodating.

All my letters now will be for you and my little son. After the entire dirt I've done you, you still amaze me by keeping my real surname for him to use. Rodney Martin Allaway ... Such a nice ring to it! Thank you.

I'm so sad that he may never know me... I'm thrice punished; by society (Which I can tolerate, because I deserve it). Then by Immy and my seven-year-old princess here in New York, which I can now tell you about (with extreme sorrow). And now, will you also slap me when I'm down by adding more separation to my already lonely heart?

I absolutely refuse to agree with your thinking about destroying all my letters, so that our son can never read them. We talked about the sonnets I have been writing. Will you at least save those? I'm planning a new one each week. Here's number one:

I sat bowed down in sad, remorseful pain
Within that place of all forgotten men,
Filled with the rush of memories again;
Thinking thoughts that drive poor fools insane,
When all at once a shaft of dazzling sun
Shone thru the bars and flooded all my cell,
Seeming to lift me from the depths of hell—
I wondered at a false joy just begun.
A vision of my past then seemed to say:
"Fear not, dear one, for beauty has not died;
Your pain is only memories magnified,
A future love will make it fade away."
The vision passed and I, with mind so slow,
Was vaguely wondering why it hurt me so!

My dear Jerry; Here's another week's offering:

The only words I know are much too crude
To act as messengers to your closed heart.
I dare not fondly trust them to impart
My tender feelings, lest they should intrude
Into your silent, peaceful solitude,
Probing your wounds until they bleed and smart,
Making you take the bitter, aching part,
A prey to feeble words, so dull and rude.
My love for you is such a constant thing—
If I could only write some quiet words,
That, like the lovely fluttering of birds,
Would softly steal within your heart and sing
Of happy days again, and skies above,
I'd send them as the messengers of love!

I'm still patiently waiting for those promised pictures. Don't fail me. You'd never realize how much they would please me.

#

My dear Jerry;

> *I can be sick to dying in my mind,*
> *With gnawing pains that press my spirits down,*
> *About my forehead in a gruesome crown,*
> *While fearful demons prick me from behind;*
> *I can be chilled to freezing in my heart,*
> *Rigid with dull despair, stark with the cold*
> *Of half-dead hopes that flutter as of old,*
> *And neither stay to comfort me, nor part.*
> *I can be lost in darkling mists, that stand*
> *As proof that grief can make a soul dumb,*
> *Fighting with vivid nothings, and my hand*
> *Striking with futile force at fears that numb,*
> *But all these ugly horrors vanish and*
> *The sun is shining when your letters come.*

That ought to soften your hard heart and make you write oftener. Maybe it would even soften you to the extent that you would deign to send a snapshot of yourself. I hope so. If a letter cheers me up to such an extent, imagine what a photo would do. Also, I expect one of Rodney soon, bless his little heart!

All my love, *Pete*

#

Summer, 1933:
My dear Jerry;
I hope this takes the "flatness" out of your life for a few minutes, at least:

> *The inspiration of my love for you*
> *Is such that, surely sometime, from above*
> *Will spring a song that's worthy of you, love—*
> *A song as purged of falsehood, and as true*
> *As matins that the feathered songsters sing.*
> *Sometime, from my fierce longing and my pain,*

123

Will rise a song to pierce your proud disdain,
And make it seem a little, selfish thing.
Sometime, my muse will surely give a sign—
Meanwhile, I think my perfect theme will keep,
Singing within my heart in strains divine,
Burned in my memory with etchings deep:
The perfect fit of arms and breast to mine,
And how you turned and kissed me in your sleep!

#

My dear Jerry;

I wrote to Immy's attorneys last week to see what's what and they replied that she had presumably dropped her contemplated action as she had recently asked the return of all papers. However, my own theory is that she is hiring a different law firm. The former ones were at a high-priced uptown address. She should be able to get her divorce without any lawyers. I certainly won't contest it.

I am very anxious to hear of the latest developments at your office. Kiss my big fella for me.

I cannot ease the burden of your fears;
Of future hopes I have no power to sing,
Nor can I make the past a little thing,
Or resurrect the joy of faded years.
No feeble words of mine can banish tears;
No crude and stilted rhyme can ever bring
The fragrant breath of sweet returning Spring,
Nor make sweet music for your hungry ears.
Why should I strive to make you hear at all?
Dreamer of dreams, born out of my due time,
Let it suffice that my insistent rhyme
Beats with light wing against this prison wall.
But should it penetrate to you, think well
Of this fond, foolish scribbler in a cell!

#

My dear Jerry;
I hope this isn't too personal:

> *I shall forget the time I could not bear*
> *To think that Spring had come again and I—*
> *Shut in beneath a gray, depressing sky,*
> *Locked up in prison where I could not dare*
> *Imagine daffodils' or tulips' flare*
> *I shall forget the time I did believe*
> *That Spring could never come but to deceive,*
> *With promise of delights, these years so bare.*
> *But now I see the brown earth turning green,*
> *And hear the wanton message of the breeze*
> *Singing within the glory of the trees*
> *Traced against the sky, blue and serene.*
> *I shall forget, Spring, that I sighed my sigh,*
> *For you have changed, it seems—or is it I?*

And after that, good night, and don't forget to send that snap of our big boy as soon as you get time.

#

My dear Jerry; Here's this week's contribution:

> *From the small bounty of your words to me,*
> *I gather every gentleness of tone,*
> *And make of them a harvest of my own—*
> *The words you've mannered somewhat tenderly.*
> *I store them in my heart's own granary,*
> *The choicest fruits that all your letters yield,*
> *Forsaking commonplaces to the field,*
> *And hold these rare delights in memory.*
> *Each night I open up my storehouse door,*

To count each precious utterance, each phrase
Worded to ease my solitary days,
I count them once again, and wish for more,
Greedy for love, wishing to hoard it all,
And wondering why my harvest is so small!

Has the rainy season stopped yet so you can take some snapshots? Please don't forget that … some of yourself too. Give my boy a big hug.

All my love, *Pete*

Chapter 14

Cape Town, South Africa
November 7, 1943

Dear Putzi:

Well, I guess this old retired G.I. is going to get to see the world, before they get me back home. When my orders finally came through in Calcutta, India, they put me on a ship to Cape Town, South Africa. Oh! Boy. I thought sure that I would go east, back through Australia, Hawaii and then to San Francisco or Seattle. But, oh no! So, I'm on a round-the-world cruise going the other way, instead.

I really had my hopes high, when I got here; planning to buy all sorts of stuff that is scarce or rationed everywhere else. First stop was going to be Woolworths or Ackermans, for some comfy undywear, scarce colognes and other good stuff. But, rotton luck followed me everywhere as all the bazaar (store clerk) employees were on strike all over the city.[9] At Woolworths, there was seventy gorgeus girls carrying pickett signs and singing songs to ukulelle and accordia music. The girls were mostly white and very pretty, but they refused to let me in the store.

They put us up in a fancy apartment suit for a whole week. But the damned grocery bazaars was also closed. I wanted to buy some real beefsteak to cook, but they had given all there perishables to charities. Even here in a huge rich city like Cape Town, the best the Army could do for us was more of them danged canned rations.

To pass the time, me and some other fellas took in movies every day. They don't allow war films here, so we had to watch stuff like *"Take A Letter Darling"* with Roslyn Russell and Fred MacMurray, or *Tennessee Johnson* with Lionel Barrymore and Ruth Hussey. The last one was better, Hedy Lamarr and Walter Pidgeon in *White Cargo*. The only movies we had in Assam were barely talkies, out of the early thirties.

One day, I took a walk down in the diamond and gold bazaars. They were too rich to be on strike. There were some great opportunities to buy stock or other investments in gold and diamond ventures. But I think that I learned a good lesson twenty years ago, and was able to avoid the tempter.

Well, kid, I can't wait to get back in your arms. While I'm waiting for a ship to the States, I sure am starved for some good red meat. Hoping you are the same, I remain,

Very truly yours, *Gomer Fudd*

P.S. The labor strikes here, remind me of another Labor Day, years ago…

#

Labor Day
September 10, 1933

Only a year ago, my dear Jerry and I were having our last talk together. I've wondered what there was about anniversaries that made them seem different than other days. Somehow or other, my memories on such a day were always more intense and poignant.

I've wished for a year that I could get over feeling the way I did about her, but I guess it was hopeless. I never seemed to have any trouble forgetting before then. I knew that it proved that it was only time I've ever been really serious in my feelings. But I also knew that she didn't care for that kind of emotional reminiscing.

So much for the monikers, John Joseph Bart, alias Guisseppe Bartisti. Officially, I couldn't even use "Pete" there at the Big House. I was stuck with the boring Basil Lawrence Allaway, #A86690. I labored in the laundry two days a week, did accounting for the warden two days a week and the rest of the time was pretty much my own to read or write in my cell.

We had an interesting field day on Labor Day with all kinds of athletic events, including a pie-eating contest. Although the rain poured down and the field was muddy, everybody seemed to enjoy himself. When I was free and employed, Labor Day was always a welcome vacation, but now is primarily a break in the everyday boredom. We learned all kinds of trivia in there, to help pass the time. Labor Day became a national holiday to honor of the working class, the celebration of it was initiated in the U.S. in 1882 by the Knights of Labor, who held a large parade right there in New York City. In 1884 the group held a parade on the first Monday of September and passed a resolution to hold all future parades on that day and to designate the day as Labor Day. Subsequently other worker organizations began to agitate for state legislatures to declare the day a legal holiday. In March 1887, the first law to that effect was passed in Colorado, followed by New York, Massachusetts, and New Jersey. In 1894 the U.S. Congress made the day a legal holiday. Parades and speeches by labor leaders and political figures marked Labor Day celebrations. You see, I had lots of time to study and do research.

The next day I saw only part of one ball game and had to return to work in the warden's office on account of a stiff wind that was blowing up which reminded us that summer was darned near over. That didn't make me mad, however, as the time passed more quickly in winter on account of the fact that we returned to our quarters at sundown which was as early at 4:20 around Christmas time. The time always moved faster when I could work or read without interruption of any sort. And then it was easier to sleep in cool weather and the time spent in sleeping was, by far, the most profitable of any in there.

No sonnets for Jerry this week; just a simple verse:

THRENODY (?)
Lilacs blossom just as sweet
Now my heart is shattered
If I bowled it down the street,
Who's to say it mattered?
If there's one that rode away
What would I be missing?
Lips that taste of tears, they say
Are the best for kissing.
*** *

Eyes that watch the morning star
Seem a little brighter;
Arms held out to darkness are
Usually whiter.
Shall I bar the strolling guest,
Bind my brow with willow,

When, they say, the empty breast
Is a softer pillow?
***

That a heart falls tinkling down,
Never think it ceases.
Every likely lad in town
Gathers up the pieces.
If there's one gone whistling by
Would I let it grieve me?
Let him wonder if I lie;
Let him half believe me.

#

My Dear Jerry: On a personal level, please don't let the hardships of this depression affect your attitudes toward life, work, and your community. So many people who struggle through the depression want to protect themselves from ever again going hungry or lacking necessities. Some will develop habits of frugality and careful saving for the rest of their lives, and many will be focused too much on accumulating material possessions to create a comfortable life, that they will forget how to enjoy life. However it turns out, though, it will be one far different from that which we have experienced these last two years.

Prison life has changed so much during the past ten to twenty years. Remember the old chain-gangs we used to see in editorial cartoons? Prisons are no longer "labor camps" like they used to be. As labor influence grew in the late nineteenth and early twentieth centuries, dramatic changes occurred. By the 1920s, labor critics, joined by the humanitarian critics, achieved their aim of severely restricting prison labor.

The U.S. Congress enacted the Hawes-Cooper Act (1929), which divested prison-made goods of the protection afforded by the Interstate Commerce Act and made such goods subject to state punitive laws. During the depression of the 1930s, Congress completed the task by prohibiting transport companies from accepting prison-made products for transportation into any state in violation of the laws of that state. This legislation, the Ashurst-Sumners Act (1935), effectively closed the market to goods made by prisoners, and most states then terminated prison industry.

Rehabilitation is now the goal of all prisons, so that's why we have some social activities, and are allowed out of our cells to work and play.

INVENTORY
Four be the things I am wiser to know:
Idleness, sorrow, a friend and a foe.
Four be the things I'd been better without:
Love, curiosity, freckles, and doubt.
Three be the things I shall never attain:
Envy, content and sufficient champagne.
Three be the things I shall have till I die:
Laughter and hope and a sock in the eye.

How is my big boy? When I see some of the little tots running around in the grandstand, I certainly get my share of heartaches. What a mess I've made of things! I do not pity myself. I only feel like kicking myself for being the worlds champion fool. However, while there's life, there's always hope, and that's all I live on now. In the meantime, be good and write often.

Always, *Pete*

#

Winter, 1933-34:
My dear Jerry;

Why should I groan, and say "What pain is mine!"
And rail against my ugly circumstance,
Wailing heartbroken in a dreary trance,
Envying the light in other eyes a-shine?
Why should I blind myself against the day,
Seeing no trace of that which men call fair,
Seeing myself a ghost with graying hair
Within this somber place where all is gray?
I wonder how my heart resists the power
Of warming comfort in the skies of blue,
Or why I cannot thrill to every flower,

131

Or song of birds just like I used to do.
I do not know why life should seem so dour,
Unless my entire world was wrapped up in you!

We had a quiet Thanksgiving, as usual. I hate holidays here, also weekends, because I'm less busy and time drags. Kiss my big boy.

#

My dear Jerry;

I had no right to take your love, my dear,
A fugitive from ghosts which I had made.
But I was very sure and unafraid,
And thought my past was peaceful in it's bier,
And I was soul-starved for that sacred thing,
Hungry for love to ease my loneliness,
Longing for something missed—a happiness
I'd never known and, hence, could never sing.
Was my offense so far beyond the pale,
When love's forbidden fruit fell at my feet—
When some sweet inner voice told me to eat?
My weary conscience does not fret or wail.
Perhaps it, too, was numbed by your bright flame!
In that case, dear, was I so much to blame?

The above is terrible, but still apropos. I am anxious for some news about my big son and his mother ... also, it's about time for some more pictures, don't you think?

Here's another weeks' contribution:

One time I wrote a closing verse to you,
Based on immortal Browning's lovely lines,
Of how our love through old age intertwines,
And guides us on the paths we must pursue.
I dare not seek the future's hidden ways

To find the love I lost so long ago;
I'm fearful that the years so sad and slow
Will leave me old with barren, empty days.
These hours of loneliness and bitter tears,
That I have nightly in my narrow cell,
Give me a foretaste of the future's hell—
Unless you come to fill those far-flung years,
And make that happy dream of age come true—
That lovely dream I wrote in rhyme for you!

Do you remember the "closing verse" referred to? Give the boy a big hug for me. I wish you'd answer some of the questions I've asked.

#

My dear Jerry;
How I miss the good life and you and my son. Do you remember how seriously that I vowed to "go straight" two days before they came to arrest me? Here's the sonnet written two years ago:

One time when I was bowed down in defeat,
A temporary fog of deepest gloom—
I longed for some cool-shadowed inner room,
And thought that only quiet could be sweet;
I longed for silent cloisters, some retreat
Where I might muse in philosophic style,
Hidden away from your disturbing smile,
Far from the life of men—far from deceit.
Now I'm alone, locked up and impotent;
I should be quiet, but my aching grief
Denies me peace to test my old belief,
With four bare walls I cannot be content.
I long intensely for my former strife,
That sweet, fierce fury of a real life!

Love to Rodney and you too, *Pete*

#

1935:
My dear Jerry;
The following, although written two years ago, expresses my present mood:

> *Sometimes I wish that I had died before*
> *I came to know the aching of desire—*
> *Before I learned to dread the scorching fire—*
> *The pulse that pounded when I neared your door.*
> *It were much better had I crept alone*
> *Into the shadow—out of love's bright beams—*
> *Better than reaping dregs of empty dreams,*
> *And drinking bitter cups while I condone.*
> *Better, perhaps, that we had never met.*
> *If there had been no joy, then there would be*
> *No futile hope, no painful memory,*
> *No bitter longing and no tears, and yet,*
> *For all this pain the gods I humbly thank—*
> *Without it life would be a dismal blank!*

I still feel that way, more or less. You can't expect me to change a great deal in here. It would be hard enough outside where I could meet civilized people of both sexes. Kiss my big son for me.

#

My dear Jerry;
How these gray walls close in on me week by week, day by day, hour by hour, minute by minute, and second by second. The following was written some time ago but is appropriate to send now … lest you forget:

> *I've waited for a photograph of you,*
> *Waited despairingly for three long years—*

134

So, is it strange that this clipped picture cheers?
It shows your hand that props our son, cut through
By unkind scissors, yet this meager clue
Brings back the memory of that gentle touch,
That tender, light caress that meant so much,
Your hands that were refreshing as the dew.
Something of dainty flowers they seemed to be,
Something of birds—a swallow's darting flight;
Those curving, sloping fingers, slim and white,
Those pale, cool hands that seem to summon me.
There's something in the magic of your hands
That holds me through the years to your commands!

How is my big fellow enjoying the streamlined bike? I'd give a year of my life gladly to be able to see him. Wish me luck. I don't believe I'll be able to stand much more of this and keep normal, if I am now.

All my love, *Pete*

#

July 19, 1935:

My dear Jerry;

Here is a recent one, not very satisfactory to me, but truthful nevertheless:

I never pen a word by night or day
Of dawns or twilight's, or of stars that shine,
Of human traits, of women or of wine,
In doleful gloom, or in glad-hearted play,
But in some wondrous unexpected way,
My love comes creeping stealthily to twine
Her fragrant memories around each line,
So I forget the things I wished to say.
I see her picture in each mystic word;
I hear her 'cello voice so sweetly clear;
Her hand guides mine, her smile if flashing cheer;
My loneliness is gone, and like a bird,

My heart is raised on some mysterious wings,
For only she can ease the dread of things!

The nightly thunderstorm is brewing, the perspiration is pouring from me as a result of the exercise of punching these keys, and my head is throbbing. In about ten minutes the deluge ... then I'll feel better. I suppose you don't have much of this kind of weather out there. Kiss Rodney for me, and write soon.

All my love, *Pete*

#

November 22, 1935:
My dear Jerry;

These ugly years, these years I live in vain,
Without a sight of loveliness to break
The dull monotony, the lasting ache,
The sodden, stupid misery of the pain.
Oh, bitter waste of years, unjust, inane—
Inhuman payment for one rash mistake;
Oh, dull eternity, when shall I wake
To see the sun shine through this endless rain?
Perhaps, if you would signify your choice
Of waiting till the end of my restraint,
I could take heart and banish all complaint,
Content that some day I should hear your voice,
And feel on grievous wounds on lonely years
The balm of welcoming and healing tears!

How is my big fellow these days? It seems ages since I last heard about him.

All my love, *Pete*

Chapter 15

Home at Last
November 21, 1943

Dear Putzi:

Well, you could never guess where I am at. I could almost walk to your house from here but cannot tell you just where it is because that is a military secret. I am writing this from the hospital where I am having a mild siege of malaria but I will be free pretty soon.

We had a nice trip around the world and reached New York about one week ago. First we traveled to Bombay and then got on a big ship which only had a few people on it some of which was women including Peggy who I mentioned before. She is an old maid but pretty nice to talk to.

I did not do any work except loaf and be corporal of the guard every third night. I had English and Chinese sergeants under me and they didn't like being bossed by a corporal but the Colonel said it was an American ship and so the Americans would take charge of all things.

We stopped at the Seychelles Islands and bought some oranges and mangos and then went to Cape Town in South Africa. That is just like a nice American city, except for what I told you in my last letter. We had lots and lots of good beer which nobody would let us pay for. From there we went to Trinidad and then Puerto Rico at which places we loaded up with troops all going home for Christmas. It feels pretty cold here after being in the tropics so long and I thought I had a bad cold but the doctor says it was malaria.

Well, he says I can get out in a day or so, so I would like to make a date with you to meet you at the Blue Banjo on next Saturday night and also bring Nellie and Margaret with you. I have a good case of the jitters and my tongue is hanging out. Hoping you are the same, I remain

Yours truly, *Gomer Fudd*

P.S. I guess this is the end of the World War II adventure; and it reminds me of another ending in another story whose span of time has narrowed now to only seven short years ago:

#

Halfway to Parole
October 12, 1936

My dear Jerry;[10]
Now, dear one, you will have no excuse for not sending pictures! Your new address on "Kodak Drive" in Los Angeles should remind you every day to use your Kodak.

It's the end of another long, weary holiday and no news. The weather has suddenly turned cold; which is good for sleeping, but not much else.

The *Hindenburg* airship that is headquartered nearby at Lakehurst, New Jersey, passed over us very low the other morning and gave us a nice view; our Black Sheep football team beat their opponents 54 to 0; and our cat had seven kittens. That's a lot to happen in just one week in here. Usually one week is so much like the other that I couldn't tell you, if my life depended on it, what happened two weeks or a month ago. Perhaps it's better, in a way. Without any landmarks of happenings the time seems shorter in retrospect. Only the future is long.

So the paucity of news calls for another sonnet:

> *It must have been her lovely flashing smile*
> *That brightened all my life, my pain-dulled eyes,*
> *I only know I felt a sweet surprise*
> *That love and I could stay with her awhile.*
> *Perhaps it was her gentle, silent ways*
> *That tried to guide me truly, but in vain.*
> *I only know that sometimes after rain*
> *I breathe the sweet perfume of other days.*
> *I have no wish to know how love occurs—*
> *For who could analyze this mystic thing?*

I only know that swallows on the wing
Could not turn swifter than my heart to hers;
I only know the brightest stars above
Could not be more steadfast than my love!

Do you like that? How is my big boy getting along? Isn't it about time for another picture (From your Kodak)? I don't want to rush you, but it's nearly six months since the last one and he must have changed a lot.

I've gazed at the snapshot of you until I could draw it from memory ... that is, if I could draw at all.

All my love, *Pete*

#

My dear Jerry;
This week's sonnet:

Oh heart, let us lie down and close our eyes
Against the cruel ugliness of bars—
Let's lose this drabness in a dream of stars,
And moonbeams sifting silver from the skies.
Let's close our ears to all the sordid sound,
And dreams of summer wind, and rain in spring,
Of trees, and mountains, and of streams that sing—
And songs of birds in melody profound.
This narrow cell can harbor wondrous dreams,
And breathless beauty soothes me in the dark—
But when I wake, a world grim and stark
Awaits my eyes—a world wherein it seems
That ruthless Beauty stands beyond the door
To taunt me with these dreams and wound me more!

Do you like that? It was written a year and a half ago, but my sentiments haven't changed. You must be about fed up with my verse by this time. Please tell me if you are... How is my big man? Are you going to send a picture soon? And when are you going to sink your pride and send one of yourself?

All my love, *Pete*

#

My dear Jerry;

Okay, if that's what you desire, I'll not send any more verse, after this one written especially for Rodney:

I might well say I do not know my son—
He was so very young when last I looked
On his sweet baby face; before Fate crooked
Her bony finger, and my dream was done.
Although the way is long, and time is, too,
Before I see you, son, please teach me now,
Teach me to grow in wisdom – tell me how
I can be worthy to be loved by you!
Teach me to know the truer, better way
To answer all your future wants; to be
A model for you in your work and play;
More thoughtful of the need you have of me—
Oh, little hand that gropes the way along,
Reach out your love to me, and make me strong!

Thanks for the Christmas pictures. I still don't know who he resembles. In some of the snaps, I see my Jerry, especially when he is smiling, but when he is sober I can see a resemblance to my family.[11] The snap you sent last summer in a sun suit was a dead image of Pete when he was a baby. Of course, you wouldn't know that. Everything is still the same here. No news, not even rumors.

So, you prefer Ronnie to Rodney? That's fine with me.

All my Love, *"Proud Papa Pete"*

#

January 13, 1939[12]

Dear Jerry;

Just a few lines to let you know that my pre-parole interviews have started, and you may expect to receive some inquiries before long. Of course, I can't avoid giving them your name as our correspondence is a matter of record. At any rate, use good judgment in answering any questions,

On the face of things just now, it looks as if I would not be permitted to go to the west unless I have a job out there, but, of course, I haven't given up the idea. It would be rather silly (don't you think?) to be forced to stay in this state for another three years and then, when my parole is finished, have to re-settle myself in the west which is my home.

What I want to do is to get settled definitely and for all time just as soon as possible. I would look on a parole period in New York as a total waste of time, unless I happened to get a real good opportunity, which isn't likely.

I am very jittery and restless … can't get my mind down to reading or work of any kind. The last few Sundays I have spent in tearing up the accumulated work of the last six years. I also tore up copies of letters to you, after reading them over, and am convinced that you must have a heart of stone not to be touched by some of the eloquent and pathetic appeals of the first year or so. I even felt sorry for myself.

These interviews I am having at the present time are not so good. After being left alone all this time, it burns me up that all of the old dirt should be dug up and pawed over. It seems so unnecessary.

Give my love to Ronnie, and write soon.

As ever, *Pete*

#

July 10, 1939

Dear Jerry;

The only reason I'm writing this note is that it occurred to me that you might think me particularly heartless at foregoing the chance to see my son, Ronnie.

As a matter of fact, it took more will power than I ever suspected myself of having. Furthermore, there was quite some fear in my mind that I wouldn't be able to stand it … that I might break down and make a fool of myself and spoil everything.

I only felt that way, of course, after your spectacular announcement *THAT YOU HAVE BEEN MARRIED!* I thought it would be best for all concerned if I just passed out of the picture.

My first impulse was to run out and get a drink about a foot high, but after a few moments of reflection, I knew if I did, that I would wind up weeping on someone's shoulder. (I assume, from all appearances, there are plenty of nice shoulders one could weep on in Los Angeles, for a consideration.) However, I went directly to the ticket office and got reservations on the train that left at 7:45 that evening then checked out of my hotel, and here I am back in Portland.

I thought that after the shock of your announcement had worn off, I would feel terribly hurt, but surprisingly enough, I don't. Thank God!

This is the last time you will hear from me, unless things change a great deal. My last real tie has been broken, and I am breaking my agreement with the state of New York.

In a few hours I shall leave for parts unknown and make a fresh start without the handicaps under which I have existed for so long. If you think this action cowardly, please consider all angles before you pass judgment. I could stand parole if there were a reason for it. That is, if I had a wife and children, a home and a good job, then I would have something that would be worth more than this elusive freedom. But, under the circumstances … the heck with it.

If anyone should inquire about me, and I'm sure that the parole board will, you are free to tell him or her everything or nothing, whatever you think best.

I only ask one favor … be good to Ronnie, and when he is old enough to discuss things, treat my memory as kindly as possible. Will you?

And now, all the happiness you deserve, and more, forever.

And, thanks for the memories! *Pete*

P.S. By the way, that crook Bill Creitz is married and has the sweetest boy, born nine months and ten minutes after they were married. I certainly had to laugh to see him changing diapers. God bless you, Jerry!

Pete

#

December 28, 1940
Greetings, and Best Wishes for a HAPPY NEW YEAR (Jerry);

> *There is a space between the change of years,*
> *A narrow moment where the heart may cast*
> *Its hope again, where all that fails or fears*
> *Dies for a little with the dying past.*
> *Now in this time of stars, in this cold night*
> *That turns the old years from us for the new,*
> *I have for you no more than mortal light.*
> *Frail and beset the thing I give to you.*
> *Be happy ... this my word that cannot reach you*
> *Whenever it would, whenever the heart is lonely.*
> *Be happy ... though my hand may never touch you*
> *In joy or love or loneliness, but only*
> *With one wish for you, changeless as a star*
> *Whatever the tide may be, wherever you are!*

#

So now, dear reader, I have fallen into the depths of depression and sometimes feel that I am trapped in a condition worse than prison ever could have been. I think that I could write a book, called either *Depression* or *How to Become an Alcoholic Without Really Trying*. How's this for an opening *foreword:*

"I had twelve bottles of whiskey in my cellar, and my wife told me to empty each and every bottle down the sink, or else ... So I said I would and proceeded with the unpleasant task.

"I withdrew the cork from the first bottle and poured the contents down the sink, with the exception of one glass which I drank.

"I extracted the cork from the second bottle and did likewise, with the exception of one glass, which I drank.

"I then withdrewed the cork from the third bottle and purred the whusky down the drink, with the exception of one glass, which I drank.

"I pulled the cork from the fourth sink and poured the bottle down the glass, which I drinked.

"I pulled the bottle from the cork of the next and drank one sink of it, and threw the rest down the glass.

"I pulled the sink out of the next glass and poured the cork down the bottle and drank the glass.

"I pulled the next cork from my throat and poured the sink down the bottle. Then I corked the sink with the bottle, glassed the drink and drank the pour.

"When I had everything I steadied the house with one hand and counted the bottles, cork, corks and glasses and sinks with the other, which were twenty-nine. To be sure I counted them again, and when they came by, I had seventy-nine, and as the house came by I counted them again, and finally had all the houses, and corks and bottles and glasses and sinks counted, except one house and one bottle which I drank. Salud."

I've moved over to Yakima, Washington, where two of my sisters and a brother live and it sounds like the world is gearing up for another nasty war… and if that happens, I think I might change my name again. How does *Don Pedro* sound, or maybe *Gomer Fudd?*

The following relates to nothing in particular, but I feel good enough to be included:

Of all the insidious
Temptation invidious
Contrived by the devil for pulling man down,
There's none more elusive
Seductive, abusive
Than the snare to a man with his wife out of town.
He gets such delightfulness, stay-up-all-nightfulness
Sure-to-get-tightfulness
(And I own it—with pain)
A bachelor rakiness, what-will-you-takishness,
Hard … to explain.
* * *
His wife may be beautiful, tender and dutiful
'Tis not that her absence may cause him delight,
But the cursed opportunity,
Baleful immunity,
Scatters his scruples as day scatters night.

\#

And...

UNFORTUNATE COINCIDENCE
If I don't drive around the park,
I'm pretty sure to make my mark.
If I'm in bed each night by ten,
I may get back my looks again.
If I abstain from fun and such,
I could really amount to much;
But I shall stay the way I am,
Because I do not give a damn.
***

Chapter 16

"Recollections of a Wandering Love"
by "Pete" Allaway

"He who desires anything will live and wander and suffer accordingly until desire is dead."
—Sanscritic Vedanta

#

Part One

This is the land of mystery and romance,
Of ticks and leeches and of flying ants,
Of bugs and cobras and anopheles,
Of much enchanted nonsense, and of fleas.
This land is old to me, and if I smile,
In this re-incarnation that's so vile,
It's that I recollect a former life
When you, a Rajah's daughter, were my wife,
And I, a wondering troubadour whose creed
Had little fear of Karma, and small heed
To Vishnu, Shiva, Brahma or the rest,
So long as I could clasp you to my breast
And break your ribs and bite your little ears
And bring a calm Nirvana to your fears.
How did I die that life? I don't recall—
We've had so many lives that this one brawl
Escapes my memory at this late date.
I only know that some religious hate
Engendered by the priests and your old man

Threw me, a wicked pagan, in the can.
No doubt my end was terrible, for now
I know the holy ones can raise a row
That make the Nazis seem like cooing doves!
Oh well, this love of all our many loves
Was part of endless Karma that the Three
Have sentenced me to suffer till I'm free
Of this desire for you. Until I seek
That blessed Nothingness of which they speak
I must go on, life after futile life
Replete with sorrow, wandering and strife.
The gods are strong, but phooey on them all—
I will not bow my head to them, or crawl—
I want no lazy state of spirit bliss,
My lust is strong for life and for your kiss—
My creed is this: To live and care not why—
To laugh, to weep, to drink, to love, to die!

#

A million years have passed since we have known
The pangs and joys of love and we have grown
Through countless ages ruled by perverse Fate,
From cavemen to this highly modern state.
Hell, I'm a caveman yet, and when I woo
I beat your pretty body black and blue,
And sate my lust with many a kick and blow
To quicken you to love and kisses so!
And you, my love, are just about as mean
As that fair morn I conked you on the bean
And laid you out and grabbed you by the hair,
And dragged you, spitting wildcat, to my lair!
I never can forget when first we met;
You, in your well-feigned innocence, my pet,
Had wandered lonely far away from home.
I bounced a boulder off your lovely dome
And knocked you flat and thought that you were dead
Until you laughed and ran—then I saw red

And caught you quickly and with loving sighs,
Kicked in your slats and blackened both your eyes—
Parted your auburn tresses with a stone—
Kicked your rear end and broke your pelvic bone,
Twisted your arm until you screamed, "Enough!"
When one loves tensely, one is sometimes rough!
Those were the Primal days; there is no tongue
Can sing of love when love was really young—
No deep-browed bard can witness to the joys
Of passion such as ours that never cloys.
Now in this lonely time my mind recalls
Our many lives—our many loving brawls,
How you would sink your teeth into my wrist,
With loving gratitude at being kissed;
You'd claw my face and pull my hair, and sigh
Profession of a love that could not die.
Those were the Primal days—Oh lovely age
When your green eyes would glow with sultry rage,
And I, perforce, must beat you to your knees,
Striving, my love, as always just to please—
Dreading the moment when we had to part.
You loved it, just as did I, my sweetheart!
You thrilled to all my loving, brutal ways—
Alas, my dear, those were the Primal days!
#
Do you remember all the bulls I threw?
Do you recall the mastodon I slew?
Remember that fierce mammoth that I landed
With just my knife of stone and single handed?
I trailed him to his dank and dismal fen
And when I had him cornered, there and then,
I gouged his eyes and brought him to his knees,
And stabbed until I heard his dying wheeze,
Cut off his tongue and other dainty meat
And cast it all in triumph at your feet.
We lived on tasty sirloin steaks for two

And varied this with pterodactyl stew.
I'd break the bones against your lovely bean
And daintily would suck the marrow clean.
Those were the days when you were faithful there,
Tamed by my love within our lovely lair,
Where you would sew my skins and cook for me,
And, incidentally, raise a family.

#

Our love, my turtle dove, was ever warm—
Your sighs, my dear, were like a tropic storm—
A playful kiss would set the woods on fire,
And make my lovesick heart a burning pyre,
A glance would melt the circumjacent snow
Where mighty dinosaurs rolled to and fro
Trying in vain their blistered hides to cool—
Burned to a frenzy in that nearby pool
Which you had turned to boiling just that morn
By contact with your fair caloric form.
Alas, it's gone—that olden time of charms
When we lay melted in each other's arms.
I still love warmly in the pallid age,
But drear convention somewhat stills my rage!

#

The gods are strong, but phooey on them all—
I will not bow my head to them, or crawl—
I'll do my bit of Karma and aspire
To nothing else but you—and my desire!

#

I sit far from the clamour of the street
Singing the miracle that we should meet
Age after age in almost every clime
Down through ten thousand centuries of time.
Bereft of your sweet presence for a while,
I recollect the olden days, and smile.
How I would wax poetic through the years
About your auburn hair, your shell-pink ears,

149

Your graceful posture and your form divine,
Your pearly teeth, your flashing smile, in fine,
Sometimes I beat you when you did no wrong—
Your charms defied my art to make a song!
#
A brontosaurus with his sluggish girth,
Grinning five fathoms broad in loutish mirth,
Looked into our cavern door and laughed
To see a lovesick caveman acting daft,
His silly laughter rolled up to the sky
To see me sing, instead of black your eye—
Just so, these modern louts who jeer and bray
To see me writing rhyme like this today!
#
Not long ago, my sweetheart, as I strolled,
I chanced upon a museum of things old,
And passed within to garner memories
Of olden days that live in reveries,
And, Oh my dear, the thrill it gave to me,
For there, plainly labeled for all to see:
"Homo Neanderthalensis—Stone Age Man,"
With battered sloping skull and grisly pan.
Behind its ear I recognized the dent
That you gave me the morning that you bent
A skillet on my head and knocked me flat
For teasing your old sabre-toothed tom cat!
The beating memories came like a surge
And with them all a mighty primal urge
To seek you out among this modern throng,
Love you and lock you in my arms so strong!
I met you, sweetheart, strolling in the park—
You were alone and it was nearly dark.
I recognized your hair, your lovely form,
Your eyes that brooded with potential storm,
I knocked you down and tied you to a tree
And bit your lovely ears in joyful glee,

150

Pressing warm kisses on your swan like neck—
A sudden pain and darkness, and, by heck,
Awoke next morning in the county jail
In durance vile without a chance of bail,
With steel bars and locks and no escape,
My love had fled and I was charged with "Rape"!
By all the gods, where did they find THAT name
For holy love like ours—that beating flame
That's burned so bright for centuries untold,
A love that never, ever will grow cold?
#
Do you remember that last cave we bought,
High on a lofty mountainside where naught
Could find this secret place, secure from harm
Where you could sleep serenely on my arm?
And how we fixed it up so nice and neat
With bear skin rugs, a boudoir for my sweet
With Adam furniture and many a glyph
To keep the spirits off and scare them stiff?
If caves could talk, what tales this cave could tell!
But that was love and everything was well.
Each day I'd sit outside and whet my knife
To guard the virgin honor of my wife,
And if a Fuller brush man came that way
I would not hesitate to maim and slay.
But one sad day, our larder being low,
I scrambled to the valley down below
To kill fresh meat and garner tasty roots
And other tid-bits to your taste, my toots.
I came back early to our cavern door—
You did not haste to meet me as before—
Another man had tasted of your charms—
I found you blissful in the iceman's arms.
You screamed and pleaded, but I plugged the came
And left you and your lover in your grave!
#

And so I roam seared by this awful fire,
Sentenced to endless Karma for desire.
The gods are strong and cruel and they play
With me and send be on my dreary way.
But that hard way, as endless as it seems,
Is brightened by the face I see in dreams.
Each lifetime now I've had you for awhile,
Basked in the sweetness of your flashing smile,
Felt your warm kisses, helped you to undress,
Beat you up soundly, thrilled to your caress.
You are the end of all desire, my sweet—
A potent heresy that I repeat.
Over and over again I have confessed
To Vishnu, Shiva, Brahma—all the rest
I want no dull Nirvana, cruel Three,
Just do your damndest for eternity!

#

Part Two

This is the land of mystery and romance,
A land where once again the wheel of chance
Has thrown a lovelorn, wandering troubadour
To seek his lost desire, and suffer more.
A land where all is old—where nothing's young,
There is no modern song I have not sung
There is no joy I have not known, or pain,
In this same Hindustan, my dear, we've lain
Locked in each other's arms so many times—
So many endless lives—so many climes.
This is the land of Karma, where the Three
Are right at home to goad my misery,
I snap my fingers in their ugly mugs,
And long for my desire among the bugs.

#

In Egypt's early days in every life,
Sometimes you were my mistress—sometimes wife,

152

But whether love was right or love was wrong,
    Always an inspiration for my song
About your shell-pink ears, your lovely hair,
    For even then, my dear, you had a flair,
For making me, by some mischievous pose,
Write pretty verse or sock you on the nose.
One time you were a princess, I your slave,
    We plighted holy troth right to the grave,
And loved and fought for many a happy day,
    Until a brother slave gave us away.
They threw your lovely body to the hogs
    And laid the bastinado on my dogs,
Made me a eunuch and I had to dwell
Within the Pharaoh's harem—it was Hell!
I'd sit and plot revenge and muse about
The good old days, when with a mighty shout
    I'd clear the forest of all enemies—
Bring the tyrannosaurus to his knees—
Cow the great reptiles with a haughty glance—
Kiss you, my sweet, or kick you in the pants!
Those were the days, the good old Pleistocene
When I was king of all—and you my queen!
            #
In Babylon I stood within the mart
Where slaves were auctioned daily, and my heart
Went still, for there you stood upon the block!
    I bid and bid right down to my last sock,
    I went in debt and pledged my family
And dragged you, snarling fury, home with me!
Your auburn hair, green eyes and lissome form
    Made me write sonnets in cuneiform.
Each morn, my pussy cat, my face would bear
    The ravages of love—a scratch or tear;
    You minded me of former lives when we
    Could love each other absolutely free,
When no conventions held us in duress—

Unfettered by this ugly modern dress—
Oh Primal days, when love was ever young
Of which no minstrel plays, no bard has sung,
Where are your charms today—where is desire
As we had once that set the world on fire?
#
The law required that you should sell your charms
Once in Baal's temple in a stranger's arms,
You went to do your duty—but liked it so
You made a habit of it for the dough.
I tied you to my chariot, my sweet,
And dragged your lovely body through the street!
#
In Judah's land I sat upon the throne,
Had many wives but always seemed alone
Until I saw you on my neighbor's roof,
Where you had posed, no doubt, for my behoof—
Naked, alluring—lying in the sun,
I gazed until my heart was quite undone,
I sent a messenger for you that day
And you came to my lonely heart to stay.
Your husband was Uriah, a Hittite,
Who I, most promptly, sent away to fight
In front line trenches where he lost his life,
And you became my forty-seventh wife.
I loved you well but something still was lacking—
In former days I'd done a bit of whacking—
Already then the times were getting tame,
I could not sock your nose or eyes, or maim
Your lovely gams, or bash you on the dome,
So somehow, sweet, I did not feel at home!
#
When Greek meets Greek e'er since the days of Troy
They spurn the girls and ask for just a boy—
But we were different in our Grecian days,
We loved each other in the natural ways—

No Lesbian love was ours, no grief nor pain
Where "deep-browed Homer ruled as his domain."
I never can forget the time we met,
I saw you on the walls of Troy, my pet,
You saw me too, and we, beneath hot skies,
"Looked at each other with a wild surmise,"
You jumped into my arms, my chickadee,
And then we fled beyond the wine-dark sea.
Old Attic Helen was not worth the rub,
Compared to you she was an awful dub!
Halcyon days were ours upon that isle,
I sang about your hair, your lovely smile,
In fact, sometimes, I thought you quite divine
When I was three sheets to in Chian wine!
But though our love was free and gay and bold
It still was tame compared to days of old.
I'd linger on the shore some nights and muse
How I could rouse your passion with a bruise,
Kick in your ribs and slap your pretty rump
And earn my kisses with a lusty thump!
#
You were a Vestal Virgin, I a Gaul
Who guzzled wine in many a tavern brawl.
I don't recall how our love came about,
Just that we loved—till Vesta's fire went out.
The priests had spied on us and we were found
And you were buried living underground.
The threw me in the Coliseum's pit
To make sport for the Red Cross benefit.
I stood half-stunned amid the raucous din,
When gates swung wide and let a lion in—
He rushed at me—I kicked him on the snout
And grabbed his tail and flipped him inside out,
And then amid the plaudits of the crowd
I thumbed my nose at Caesar and aloud
I loosed my awful atavistic yell,

155

Knowing that life without you would be hell!
Angry lions rushed at me, but yet,
I could not die—but soon I raised a sweat.
How could they kill me with such puny game,
A mighty Nimrod who was known to maim
The awful mammoth with a single stroke;
The lions—and the Romans—were a joke!
But still the end was nigh, and bitterly,
I realized how drink had weakened me.
The thirty-seventh lion got me down,
And pummeled me and bit me on the ground
And I was gone—but, Oh that precious dream
When rushing thoughts of you, my sweetheart, seem
Like all eternity. I dreamed that I
Was being smothered by your loving sigh,
Some Fleeting seconds just before I died
I thought that I was lying by your side
And you were loving me in your old way
With kisses, bites and scratches just for play!

#

Do you recall, sweetheart, the first crusade?
I was a noble knight and you my maid,
And when I went to fight beyond the sea
I forged a heavy band of chastity
With heavy steel spikes and sharpened tips
And locked the whole contraption on your hips
To guard your wifely honor all the time
From wandering troubadours with thoughts like mine!
That was the last time I could truly state
That I was lord and master—not just mate!

#

The gods are strong—but phooey on them all—
I will not bow my head to them, or crawl—
My creed is this—to live and care not why—
To laugh, to weep, to drink, to love, to die!

#

156

Part Three

This is the land of mystery and romance,
Of ticks and leeches and of flying ants—
This is the primal land in miniature,
So decadent that one cannot be sure.
Just now a flying cockroach on my ear
Nibbled a message of the yesteryear
When you would bite my ears in playful fun
To wake me up before the rising sun.
And this small bug descended from the flea
That bit me in the year thirteen B.C.
This is the primal land, but it is dead
And naught remains but atavistic dread
Of mighty dinosaurs that roam no more,
Reptilian fish that terrorized the shore—
Volcanic wrath and tidal waves so vast
And other vital things that filled the past
And made a perfect setting for a love
That scorned the world, and spurned the gods above!
A love so bright, that when we lay embraced
The very earth would slacken in its haste
And time stood still, so that a flash of light
Would seem as endless as a lonely night.
Vast, winged saurian's hovering overhead
And dinosaurs that browsed about our bed
Would pause in trembling wonder at the fire,
That searing flame enkindled by desire
That's burned so steadily through centuries
And lives today within our memories!
#
Our love is old—but dreams are ever young—
'Twas just last night that our lips met and clung
And served, at my dull waking hour, to teach
How far one whispered word of love may reach
Across the vastness of infinity—

157

Down through the eons of eternity!
Surely they pass—your beauty and my rhyme,
But our love triumphs over space and time!
..oOo..

Chapter 17

Duty Section Leader
Summer, 1953

Dear Pete:

After I got you moved into the Sandy Apartments and employed at Cascade Accounting Service, I worried about how to keep you on the dry straight and narrow. Keeping your depression under control is a great challenge, but I know you can overcome it, especially with the help of your new lady. Keep yourself busy and challenged in your job, and the booze will become less and less important.

The last sonnet you sent to Mom, the one about me; *"I might well say I do not know my son..."* is a treasure that I will keep forever and someday publish in a book. Thank you for convincing Jerry to save most of your writings for me.

You should know that all your writing ability has had some influence on me. Something happened on the base the other day, so here is my dramatic version. Let me know what you think...

Duty Section Leader

The city was quiet and still; Main Street was as deserted as the out-of-the-way side streets. A bare handful of individuals were about; an occasional drunk, wondering what had happened to the Saturday night throngs; a lonely policeman, patrolling a still lonelier beat.

Far out in the suburbs, a cock crowed, heralding the approach of a silver dawn, and with it, a quiet Sunday morning of worship.

The populace was awakening, the last drunk finding his way home. The policeman's beat was not so lonely now, as early risers began their work of the day; a new day which had just dawned over El Centro, California.

I was barely conscious of a tremendous roar, very close. I heard this roar many times before during my tour of duty at the Naval Auxiliary Air Station, six miles from El Centro. It was the roar of a squadron of F9F's warming up for early morning gunnery practice. The military target areas of the Chocolate Mountains in southern California were scheduled to take another bombing.

The sound became a high-pitched scream, but even then, was not too disturbing, as military men become used to many noises of war. This noise was a repeat of noise heard every morning. Ordinarily, I would roll over in my sack and again seek immediate sleep. This morning, however, was different, I had plenty to do.

Reveille had not yet been held on the duty section, for the sun was not quite over the eastern mountains. Sheer conscientious duty rolled me out of my bunk into a barracks, still sticky from yesterday's heat. The old wood frame building shook with vibrations as the F9F sound waves smashed into it from only yards away. .

Disgruntled, I opened an eye, beholding a strange sun rising over a seemingly strange world. I had stepped into an open doorway, seeking an elusive cooling breeze and relief from the stuffy heat of the barracks.

Funny thing, I thought, *How awe inspiring is the atmosphere of the early morning.*

Faint reflections of the first beams of sunlight glittered on the wing tanks of the four aircraft, which were now taxiing up the runway, soon to leave the base in welcomed silence.

With a last breath of clean fresh air, I resigned myself to the tasks of the day. I was petty officer of the duty section and needed to get an early start. *After all, I had to set a good example for my crew.*

I woke the watch, so he in turn could get up the rest of the duty section, then I proceeded to chow.

The F9F's had by now gained sufficient altitude to circle to the east, over the city and on to their targets in the Chocolate Mountain gunnery range.

I began my breakfast with pleasure filled thoughts of eating at leisure to enjoy every bite. This was not to be. I vaguely became aware of a siren, starting low-throated at first, but rapidly graduating to a high-pitched scream. It was the siren on the operations tower, which I recognized immediately. It could mean only one thing: Crash!

Leaving my untouched ham and eggs for the flies, I was out of the chow hall even before the loudspeaker blurted forth with orders for the duty section

160

to muster at quarters. One of our noisy F9F's of a few minutes earlier had been forced down—in a fireball—right in the middle of downtown El Centro!

It was one of those horrible "nightmare" days of trauma that is never forgotten. There was nothing to be done for the unlucky pilot, or for the curious drunk, or for the lonely policeman. Our job now was to assist with mopping-up operations, and the removal and bagging of body parts.

A mangled and charred mass of metals, fibers and pulp were all that remained of the F9F and its pilot. All during our dirty task, we kept expecting my boss, the officer of the day, wondering where he was, and why he did not think this situation serious enough to demand his presence and command.

Somehow, we managed to get the job done without him and at three that afternoon, we returned to the base, tired, dirty, hungry and quite discouraged at writing up all the reports that should have been done by our commissioned officer.

Time passed and the wounds of this trauma began to heal, but pre-dawn no longer holds an inspiration for me, and I know nothing but trepidation when I see the early morning sun reflecting off an F9F wing tank.

You see, we had learned the reason for what we assumed to be my duty officer's neglect of duty. He had been the unlucky unidentified pilot!

Your Son, Ronnie "Al" Allaway
From another war

Endnotes

[1] America At War Series, *World War I*, by Peter Bosco, Facts On File Books, 1991.

[2] *Illustrated Encyclopedia of World War I*, Vol. 3 by Marshall Cavendish 1984

[3] Whites and Blacks in the military were strictly segregated into their own separate units, except aboard large vessels. This policy did not change until near the end of WW2. Pete had a photo of the entire crew of *Huron* (some 440 men and officers) and about ten were Negro.

[4] This war sonnet called "Safety" was written by Rupert Brooke. It is unclear whether or not Pete intended Immy to think that he personally wrote it.

[5] *World War 1,* Vol. **8,** Marshall Cavendish

[6] Quotation of Buddha

[7] A military tabloid, *C.B.I. Roundup* dated September 30, 1943

[8] Indictment and trial information from the archives of the Portland *Oregonian* during August, September and October, 1932

[9] *The Cape Argus*, Cape Town Daily for Monday, November 8, 1943.

[10] All Pete's letters were lengthy, like this one or longer, but my mother, Jerry, was so upset with him that she cut out most of the leading letter parts, and saved only some of the sonnets. She warned him she would do that, and he begged her not to (Spring 1933).

[11] A complete family history has been published and is available at the Yakima Valley Genealogical Society library in Yakima, WA. Published by author Rodney M. "Al" Allaway, it is 122 pages, titled *ALL-WAYS... an Allaway Family* A history of Westward Migration.

[12] It is assumed there were letters written during the long interim between December 1936 and January 1939, but none were found. It is probable that Jerry tore them up in her anger. Any affection that either one had for the other is also apparently waning.